I0682499

Secrets by Moonlight

BY

S. L. MCMULLIN

ISBN 978-1-960375-00-1
ISBN 978-1-960375-01-8

To my family; Ross, Jenna, Liam, Quinn, and Lyla,
who encouraged me to go for my dreams,
and stayed patient while I worked relentlessly
to make them come true.

Table Of Contents

Secrets by Moonlight

BY

S. L. MCMULLIN

R & S Publishing

CHAPTER 1

HOME AGAIN

The long blackout curtains lining the wide bedroom window are open a crack—the bright morning sun shining through like a laser beam, mesmerizing and inviting. I can't stop staring at it. Or maybe I lack the desire to try. Which, as of late, seems to be the norm.

Blaming the infamous early-rising sun for my idle state would be the obvious thing to do. Or on the early birds outside the window and their obnoxious, operatic chirping happening as frequently as my heartbeats. But sadly, they are not the reason I remain unmoved, unmotivated by the potential delights of the day.

Giving effort means so much more than removing oneself from the warmth and security of the blankets. Accepting the day has begun means I have to admit I had finally done it—moved back home and left him and his world behind. The life I had known for the past two years would truly be over.

It doesn't help either that my life is presently stored away, taped up tight in boxes, and stuffed in bags scattered about the cabin—my new home.

Rapid, rhythmic vibrations against the top of the nightstand beside me suddenly threaten the very demon I wish to avoid.

Slowly turning my head, I stare at my phone, contemplating the physical effort it would take to answer it. Ignoring it would be so easy. Effortless really.

The buzzing stops. Without the single pulse of a left voicemail, I sink into relief, happy to avoid reality for a little longer.

But when the quick three buzzes of a text message soon follow, my fate is sealed.

Rolling over, I reach my arm out from under the covers. A wave of prickling goosebumps travels down my arm and under the blankets, consuming my whole body. Then, with my phone in hand, I thrust it back under the covers and shiver-shake as I sit up and arrange the blankets around my head and body, only my face visible.

The phone, gripped in my hand, buzzes persistently again.

"You better get up, sleepyhead!" flashes on the phone's screen. Before it disappears, I tap it and press the phone icon.

"Just so you know, I am awake," I say in a shivery, raspy huff the moment the call connects.

"Yeah, sure sounds like it!" Jamie snorts. "Sooo, whatcha doin'?"

"Oh, you know, enjoying subzero temperatures in the cabin this morning."

"Sleeping in the nude again, are we?" She laughs.

"Cute! Very funny." I roll my eyes even though I know she can't see it. "The thermostat malfunctioned, I think." Another stint of goosebumps tingles across my body as if prodding me to find out why.

"Yikes, I thought that would be the first thing you'd check! Bitter nights in the heat of summer and all."

Sucking in a deep breath, I rush out of bed, take my blankets still wrapped around me, and dash into the hall to the box on the wall. Examining its continually changing digital face from 9:15 am to 64 degrees, I let out an exasperated huff, my eyes narrowing on the word HOLD.

"Nope," I grumble. "Just stupid me not checking the pre-programmed settings." And then I push the temperature up to 74.

Running back to my bed, I jump under the covers. The sting of the cold hardwood floor lingers on the pads of my feet as I snuggle them up tightly.

"So, you got any plans today?" Jamie asks.

"That depends; you working all day?"

"Sorry," she says quietly. "I promised Marge I'd help with that wedding and reception I was telling you about."

"Eh, it's fine." I eye the boxes by the door and on the desk against the wall with contempt. "I'll probably be unpacking anyway."

"What time you end up getting in last night?"

"Late," I say heavily. "I didn't plan on construction leaving Seattle. And then there was an accident outside Missoula. It took like two hours to go five miles. And, of course, I don't know why, but I decided to unpack the car."

"Ugh. Well, at least you made it."

"Yep, back in good old Montana," I sigh.

4

"Ouch! Don't go hiding your excitement for my sake," she adds snarkily. "But I guess it's hard being happy about something you never wanted to do in the first place."

"Jamie, that's not fair!"

"But true, just the same, isn't it?"

"Not at all! I do want to be here. You know that."

"Yeah, but also, you don't."

"Jamie."

"Okay, look, I'm just saying I get how hard it was for you to leave everything you loved there and return to nothing. But you should at least own up to it."

She's not wrong, but when she says it like that, it pains me to admit it.

"Yeah, well . . . maybe," I say quietly. "Maybe I did kind of have a bit of a meltdown about it last night."

"See! There you go. Not easy. I knew it wouldn't be! And girl—I told you to call me when that happens!"

While scrunching my knees to my chest, the blankets closed around me, I smell the distant burning of lint from off the coils of the heating system as it kicks on full blast. It takes me back to

5

another time and place altogether.

As warmth slowly thickens in the air, I let out a weighted breath. "I just didn't want to bother you so late."

"Pshaw, sleep's overrated. Besides, I was probably up doing my nails anyway."

I smirk, loving her unrelenting devotion, but I also know sleep is her one true companion.

"Anyway, it doesn't matter now because I'm fine."

"But you weren't. I mean, that's why you moved home, right? For my help?"

"Yes, but not with every itty-bitty two a.m. meltdown, especially when you have work in the morning."

"Uh, yeah! Besties are meant for those," she adds. "Hey, that reminds me, did you get your picture back before you left—like you wanted?"

The word *no* sticks to my tongue, lingering there as if out of verbal reach.

Pulling in a deep breath, I let it out slowly. The warm fuzzies I had been clinging to for dear life vanish like the flames of a blown-out candle.

"Are you kidding me?" she growls. "I told you not to let him keep it!"

"Hey, I tried! But I just couldn't make myself

ask."

"Uh, yeah, you could have! You sketched the damn thing."

"Yeah, but I don't need a reminder of all that's happened hanging on my wall, do I?" I say, my throat tightening.

I hear Jamie breathing hard through the phone like a bull ready to charge.

"Fine," she grumbles, "but Jackass Jared sure as hell doesn't deserve it either."

"Maybe not. But what would you have me do, trash it?" I say as a mixture of anger and grief rush at me from being forced into thinking of doing such a thing. "I had no other choice, so it's okay, really."

"No, it's not. None of this is. I mean, come on! What kind of low-down piece of crap does that kind of thing? Don't get engaged if you can't keep it in your pants!"

"Jamie," I say quietly as a tear travels down my cheek. "I don't want to get into this right now."

"Why? Because I'm right!"

I know her bitterness isn't directed at me, but my heart still aches because of it.

"After what's happened, can you honestly say it was worth it?"

I breathe forcefully and let out a thick, "Yes,

7

and you know why."

"Nuh-uh! Don't you dare try to feed me that garbage about you being a better person because of it! And don't for a second think that anything that jerk did makes you who you are. You were awesome well before he came along, and we all know it!"

"What about the money, then? I saved loads more than I could have ever gotten working around here."

"Ah, money," she sighs dreamily. "Such a wondrous prize for betrayal." Then she mumbles, "Sounds about right with a corporate scumbag involved."

Unable to fight it, tears well in my eyes, and I sniff.

Dang it, I didn't want to start crying!

"Shae, I-I'm sorry. I didn't mean—"

"You think I haven't already overanalyzed every bit of the last two years, Jamie? Because, trust me, I have. The lies and sneaking around. How could I have not seen it?" I say, my voice cracking under the weight of my emotions. "—the anger, the frustration, the pain I've felt because of it all. It practically consumed me. You know that better than anyone. And I don't want to hold on to it anymore." I sniff away another bout of tears, but the

8

rigid, painful lump in my throat stays. "I just can't."

She is quiet for a moment, and I am glad. I need to get control again.

"I really am sorry," she says, her soft voice carrying heavy guilt. "I just get so worked up about it, you know? He did this to you—caused all this pain! And I can't take any of it away for you. I feel so helpless. So-so useless!"

I cry harder, squinting my eyes shut tightly. I love her so much, her strength to fight for me when I have none left. "I-I know." I sob. "But you do help me. Know that, okay?"

"I promise to try harder. And I won't mention it again, I swear!"

"Mh-hm," I accept quietly.

There is a moment's pause before she cautiously asks, "Did I tell you Lainey talked with me yesterday?"

"Oh yeah?" I say with forced eagerness while wiping the tears from my cheeks. "How's she doing?"

"Actually, business is great! She wanted me to tell you she's looking for help at the bookstore if you're interested."

"Um, yeah, that could be fun, I guess."

Working would help distract me from how

messed up my life is now.

"She said to stop by the store sometime today if you can. I think you should go for it. It'd be good for you."

"Yeah. Yeah, maybe I will."

"Good! Crap, I better get back; Marge's giving me the stink eye," Jamie mumbles into the phone like she's trying to swallow it.

I laugh. "I highly doubt that."

"You're right—she loves me too much." She then snickers. "Hey, listen, do yourself a favor and don't spend all day cooped up inside, huh?"

"And waste such a good day?" I say with genuine fervor.

"Hah, I knew Glade Fever would strike the minute you got back. It's, like, impossible for you to stay away." She laughs. "I tried to get up there a few weeks ago but got stuck in the snow halfway up the mountain. I bet it's all gone now, though, with the hotness finally showing up and all."

"You think you can break away tomorrow for lunch?"

"Celie's at one?"

"Of course," I say, as if it should be obvious.

"Oh, hey, remind me later to tell you about the recent P-Burg gossip I learned. It's killer!" Jamie says operatically. "Later."

Shaking my head slowly, I toss the phone next to me on the bed. Oh, how I've missed the buzz of our small-town gossip brigade. Good or bad, they always had juicy stuff to tell.

Immediately, I recoil, remembering how hard I'd worked to keep the most heartbreaking and embarrassing moments of my life from those quick to spill them.

No, thank you. Leave me out of it.

Relenting to fate, I dress, have breakfast, and then start unpacking a few of the smaller boxes in the living room.

The old, weathered, wooden floors creak as I move about the rooms. They carry with them that aged, earthy sort of forest smell that makes me feel right at home. Taking off the white sheets from the couch, loveseat, and armchair in the living room, I am pleasantly surprised to find them in decent condition. Their retro, flowery brown upholstery and the mismatched chairs around the small, wobbly-legged square table in the kitchen aren't as bad as the alternative.

Living here means I don't have to live with my parents again. No nosey nates having to know my every move, my every intent—lovingly, of course.

No roommates to steal my things. No bathroom hogs. No food mysteriously going missing. No one to tell me I can't do the things I love doing. And the absolute best part about living on my own is the wide-open forest across the road, just waiting to be explored. I can come and go as I please; it sounds like heaven.

I spend about another hour and a half arranging, and then rearranging the furniture in the living room several times. Of course, I eventually concluded them best where they had started from, so I dragged them all back. The long couch is against the window by the front door, the armchair to its left with an end table between them, and the long coffee table out front. My pathetic 19" flat-screen TV on a small, knee-high, square table in the corner is the only addition to the room. It's not ideal, but I only watch a little anyway. Nothing compares to a good book.

Being about as settled in as I can handle, I leave the rest for later and make lunch. As I eat, eager excitement slowly comes to life inside me. Like the comfort of home, the Glade calls to me, begging me to get off my lazy bum and get there as fast as my beat-up silver Corolla can take me. Glade Fever, indeed.

12

Hidden? Yes. Old? Even more so. And yet it is anything but a simple spot among the trees. It is my absolute favorite place to be—tucked out of sight and surrounded by towering mountains. My father and I had found it when I was young on one of our many four-wheeler adventures on my uncle's property. Having been promised exclusive rights to it as long as he owned the land, I would venture there as often as I could get away. Over time it became my hideaway, my sanctuary from the harsh world of junior high and high school—my somewhere to go to clear my head. After such a long absence, I desperately crave its comfort, especially with recent events.

Unable to deny the pull any longer, I hop in my car and head north to the edge of town. A few miles out, the paved road turns to gravel the deeper into the thick forest I drive. The steeper and windier the trail gets, the more the wheels bump and bounce off large rocks and dips in the pothole-ridden road.

The familiar shakiness of the tires sends my heart pattering with anticipation. Until this very moment, I hadn't truly felt like I was home.

The unaltered scenery from my past blurs by me like an abstract painting. The luminous greens from the trees and grasses blend in with the neon reds, yellows, oranges, and purples of the Montana wildflowers like paintbrush smudges on the world's most enormous canvas, preserved and untouched forever. And the stillness is intoxicating.

The slow familiarity of the drive makes my mind wander, first with thoughts of the past, then, with it, my future. What smacks me right in the face is the harsh reality that I no longer have any ounce of what I would call a future—not the one I would choose for myself anyway. If I could, I would go back two years and tell the senior me not to sweat the daunting high school worries of test scores, scholarships, and college applications. But instead, warn me of a not-so-distant future where I'd feel the worst heartache I'd ever known. I wouldn't hesitate to say something. Future consequences be damned.

As I keep driving and reflecting, I notice the steepening of the road, a shift of chill in the air. The trees become denser, so thick I can't see anything beyond them but a hundred more tall, twisted tree trunks for what seems like forever. Two more switchbacks from now and up and over a small hill at the top of the mountain, and I will finally be "home." My sanity wrapped up in awe-inspiring seclusion.

Sometimes a person's perspective about a memory can warp with time and separation. In a way, becoming so transfigured that when seen again, it doesn't even come remotely close to resembling what it once was.

Yeah, this isn't one of those times. Everything looks so much brighter and more spectacular with time. It takes my breath away.

The clearing sits in a bowl surrounded by monumental green and brown speckled mountain ranges, their towering, jagged shapes trailing like a clawed hand of protection. They always make me feel part of something bigger than myself. The sky-high evergreens at the edge of the clearing loom over the sprightly, new growth. Their dark needles, a rich, penetrating green, seem to enhance the gleaming, bright greens of the clearing rather than deter it. And the flowers, more abundant than the roadside, are like a blanketed spectrum of oxides and fiery scarlet as far as I can see.

Like finding a favorite toy from my youth, all the good times I've had here come flooding back.

The thought occurs to me as I get out of the car and start for the meadow—I'd never leave this place if I thought no one would come looking for me.

The wind through the trees makes a steady

rumble, growing louder, then softer like ocean waves crashing on a rocky shore. Noisy yet oddly soothing. And with those waves comes the full-bodied, rich scent of pine. I breathe it in deep. The fresh, crisp air fills my lungs.

Like always, I lie on the ground in the middle of the meadow with my hands cradling my head. Fast-moving, bushy white clouds travel across the deep navy-blue sky overhead—nothing but me and the pine-filled breeze. For a moment, I feel euphoric. Free. Open to the idea of anything. Sort of how I used to feel, thinking of what life would be like after high school.

But the nonsensical illusion crumbles the second I recall, in painful detail, the exact reason for my newfound freedom.

Anguish—burning like an out-of-control wildfire—rips through my heart. Tears drip down my face and saturate parts of my auburn hair, but I don't care. I don't care about much these days, and that's the problem. When you have everything you've ever wanted, ever dreamed of, and someone rips it away without warning or consent, what's left to have concern about?

I did try to forget—to shut out the pain. But the last stage of grieving seems to taunt me wherever I go. Digging its sharp, nastily hurtful claws into my heart as if to fuse with it and never let go, no matter how hard I try to rip it free.

Desperate to find peace, I had been convinced a change in geography would be enough. But it was a lie.

How can I accept that this is my life now, alone and broken, right back to where I was two years ago? With nothing to show for it but a fractured heart that may never heal and some major trust issues, I'm not even sure therapy could correct.

Jamie was right about most of it. The money, though helpful, hardly seems worth it when you compare it to what feels like a whole lot of wasted time and unimaginable regret. I know there isn't anything I can do or say or even sacrifice to get back what I once had (not that I would want it anyway, knowing what I know now), but at least I had direction. I knew what was supposed to happen next: marriage, more college, maybe a new house, kids, and so on. Now, everything seems so uncertain. What to do, where to go, how to live? The unknown I am faced with now scares me to death.

Overwhelmed, I inhale rapidly, yet I cannot catch my breath.

Hand to my chest, I clutch it to get control.

No! I can't let it reclaim me—the panic, the all-consuming anguish. Not now! Not when I am home. Nothing can hurt me here.

I breathe deep again—then deeper.

Dang it, Shae, get control!

No matter how frustrated I feel or how hard I want to have done things differently, I can't change anything. No one can. Whether I had a say in it or not, my path in life is set. Shouldn't it finally be time I embraced it?

Crack!

The lucid sound echoes through the silence like a firecracker, followed by the weighted thud of a heavy object falling to the ground.

Like a prairie dog popping its head out of a hole in the earth, I peer above the tall grass, a breath caught in my throat. Motion at the base of an abnormally wide tree beyond the meadow's border catches my attention. Wild assumptions from harmless rabbit to aggressive, territorial moose stir in my mind. I do not move.

Peeking in and out of view, a giant, fat brown beaver gives a quick double tug at something hidden from view. Relief instantly blankets me. With another hard pull, the long, thick branch the animal has been working on breaks free and propels the creature backward.

As it drags the branch across the forest floor, the sluggish shoosh-shoosh of leaves makes me smile. I'm such an idiot. Of course, it would be something as unthreatening as a beaver and its tree.

Exhaling a loaded sigh, I collapse back to the earth but am stopped short by the rapid shimmers of light flickering across my face. A round, coin-like piece of metal is masked in the dirt beside me. It does not come loose from its muddy stronghold willingly. Finally surrendering, the treasure brings a clump of dark mud and a long silver chain.

Cleared of grassy muck, archaic, tally-like etchings are soon unveiled on its surface and bordered by a sort of braided pattern—a style somewhat familiar to me. On the back is the image of a large wolf's head. Dirt caked in its deep grooves makes it stick out like a black rock in white sand. Dirty yet beautiful.

But how did it get here?

The weight of the day drags me down like a heavy, heartache-filled blanket. And the desire to contemplate the necklace's existence diminishes as I slip it around my neck and lie back down. The chilled metal against my skin sends goosebumps down my arms as the warm sun flashes, dancing fiery red flames of light across my eyelids when it peeks in and out of the clouds above. It calms me even more.

With the help of the soothing whispers of the wind through the trees, I drift off to sleep.

* * *

The image before me is out of focus, contorted by the wispy waves of white mist all around me. Slowly, the wall of white disperses, and I find myself standing at the far edge of the clearing. Thick cloud cover blocks the sun, leaving a halo of blue sky directly overhead. The soft breeze flicking my hair into my face feels so real I can smell the earthy scent of pine it carries. Yet I know it cannot be real, for the flowers and tall trees around me remain motionless, frozen in the hollows of time.

Across the field appears a woman. Standing tall, her long, dark hair ripples in the wind around her shoulders. Her dress, as white as the tiny, delicate wildflowers around us, undulates about her ankles.

She beckons me to come to her.

I do not move.

Sh-she couldn't possibly mean me.

She waves, motioning me to move forward. When I do not, she takes a step toward me. As if having taken twenty, she is close enough now that I can see two deep dimples in her cheeks as she grins.

Again, she signals with her hand for me to come.

I want to obey, but my feet will not.

Worry, fierce and bright, shifts in her big eyes, replacing the smile on her face. She thrusts her hand out with assertion, begging me to take it.

Thunder booms intensely all around us. Black clouds now consume the sky.

With another step closer, she is right in front of me now. I can see the vibrant gold and green rings rounding the dark of her eyes.

"Who are you?" I whisper.

Her gleaming smile returns as she tentatively reaches out her hands to me once more, cupped one over the other like a closed box.

I hesitate, unsure if I should accept the secret she offers.

Steadily, she removes the hand on top. Nestled neatly in her palm is a necklace matching the one I had just found.

Feeling for the one around my neck, I am

surprised to find it missing.

"I don't understand," I say to the woman. "What do you want from me?"

Gently and with the warmest of touches, she takes my arm, lifts my hand, and places the necklace in it. Simultaneously, monstrous thunder booms around us like the heavy beats of a thousand drums.

A woman appears at the other end of the clearing. Though significantly younger than the one beside me, she still carries a familiarity about her—hair color and beauty like the one by me now.

The stranger, tall and rigid, takes an apprehensive step toward us.

The woman in white gasps and grips my arm still in her hand, making me wince in pain.

We watch as the stranger takes another step toward us. Then another and another, but she fails to advance as freely as the other woman had.

"Quickly!" the woman in white says, her thick Irish accent making it hard to understand what she is saying. She pulls me close. "You must put it on." Then she takes the necklace from me and clasps it around my neck. Just as the metal touches my naked flesh, a flash of lightning illuminates the darkened sky. It's so bright, my eyes sting. Thunder crashes so deafeningly that I can feel it through my bones.

The young woman falters in step when she sees what we are doing. Her eyes widen as she lets out an animalistic growl so powerful and full of raw rage that it contorts her beauty away.

I hardly have time to process what is happening before she suddenly charges us at full speed, her jaw clenched tight, murder in her eyes.

The woman in white shoves me away and yells for me to "Run!"

Never looking back, I sprint for the car. But the harder I run, the farther away I seem to be. My feet slip on the wet vegetation as though going the wrong way on a greased, one-way conveyor belt.

Massive drops of water plink off the top of my head. The cold chill of it travels down my cheeks. They fall faster and heavier so that by the time I finally reach the perimeter of the car, I am dirty and drenched from head to foot.

The hostile woman is upon me now. I can hear her huffing and grunting with desperate, determined vigor.

I thrust out my arm, the car's handle so close to my outstretched hand I can almost feel its cold, hard metal. And yet the pull backward keeps me from making contact.

Growling in frustration, I strain further to get what I desperately want.

The woman extends her slender arm, fingers reaching to grab me the moment mine wrap around the handle.

My eyes flutter open. With labored breathing, I stare up, blinking rapidly, as a rain shower pours down on my face.

What happened? Did I make it—am I safe?

Recognition shifts in my mind, and I remember where I am: on my back, in the meadow. The sound of more thunder pounds above me as if to mock me for forgetting.

Slowly, I sit up, panting, and scan the clearing, half expecting to see the women from my dream still there. But no woman in white. No angry one advancing. Only an empty field, the aftermath of a setting sun surrounded by storm clouds, and me, cold and drenched, hearing nothing but the patter of rain on the earth and the sound of my pounding heart in my ears.

Back at the car, I climb inside and read the clock on the dashboard—9:42 p.m.

In the driver's seat, I close my eyes and breathe—in, out, and in again, deep and unsteady.

My body feels heavy, weighed down by fatigue despite the afternoon of rest. I drape my arms over the steering wheel, my forehead resting on them. Water from my hair drips onto the seat and floor of the car with a fast, steady, tap-tap rhythm. The adrenaline from the dream still courses through my veins like a river of dread. I try to meditate it away, yet my thoughts run wild. The continual rainfall hammering loudly on the car's roof only adds to my turmoil.

The chill of the rain seeps into me, so I turn on the car and let it idle, the heat on high. The humming rumble of the running engine and the high-pressure air coming out of the vents are the only things I hear.

Looking through the rain-covered foggy windshield, I watch and wait, expecting to see the women reappear. I never do.

Never has a dream felt so real. The fear, my heart beating so fast in my chest, all of it so life-threateningly real that even now, I'm unsure if I believe it to be as simple and innocent as a dream.

Eventually, the heavy rain recedes to a soft drizzle, making the descent back down the mountain possible.

The eerily dark road lit by water-soaked

headlights is slippery and wet, with shallow puddles and deep, water-filled eroded cracks down the middle. My heart pounds nervously in my chest. My fingers clutch the steering wheel tightly. The wheels keep sliding and losing traction on the turns whenever I suddenly break. Slowly, carefully, I go down the mountain. By the time I reach the cabin, it's pushing 11 o'clock. My hands are numb, and my nerves shot.

Not having an appetite, I go without dinner.

Moving past the thermostat, I double-check it, not wanting a repeat of this morning. Then I tug the curtains closed tight in my room and crawl into bed. A pile of wet, muddy clothes lay at the foot of the bed, forgotten until morning.

As I close my eyes, I feel the heavy weight of exhaustion spill over me. Sleep quickly overtakes me.

CHAPTER 2

HARDER THAN IT LOOKS

The heavy wooden back door to the kitchen closes with a bang, its squeaky, coiled hinges retracting rapidly.

After unpacking in the living room and kitchen, I stash the recyclables in the bin and proceed to the bedroom.

In under an hour, the remainder of my things—books, pads of paper full of sketches, and several medium-sized boxes of colored chalk, charcoal pencils, and pastel crayons—are nestled on the small bookshelf on the side of the bed. Shirts hang in the tiny closet, pants and shorts stacked on the shelf above, with all five pairs of my shoes below.

Satisfied with my productive morning, I plop onto the couch in the living room and stare out the window happily.

I like it here. It's quiet. Peaceful.

Branches on the trees growing along the cobblestone path outside the yard sway in the slight breeze. Watching them, I inattentively fidget with the pendant around my neck. The markings trail under my fingertips like braille.

Raising the pendant into the brilliant sunlight, I adjust the angle, making glimmering Cobalt blue sparkles shimmer all around. For a moment, I get lost in its glittering mystery.

I had discovered the gem, fashioned to the center of it, earlier while cleaning it. And from my many summers working at the jewel shops in town, I conclude that this little beauty is anything but a cheap knockoff, worth more than I dare say aloud.

And yet, it isn't the gem that intrigues me the most; it's the markings.

Grabbing the open laptop for the coffee table, I type *types of lined symbols* in the search engine at the top of the page. Sewing patterns and engineering images appear. I then type *Languages that use symbols. Vinca, also known as old English* is at the top of the list. At a glance, nothing matches, so I try again. *Egyptian hieroglyphics.* And though pictures are used to depict stories, they don't even come close to matching.

Then I see the sub-topic *Irish lineage and folklore*, and I hesitate; the dream and the woman's accent come to mind.

Could it be that easy?

I click the link. An endless list of articles pops up, and I cringe.

Clothing. No.

Dance style. No.

Fun things to do on your vacation in Ireland. No, not right now, anyway. Pin that for later.

Gaelic Markings. Bingo! Blah, blah . . . *Celtic language* . . . blabbity blah, blah . . . *Western Gaelic* . . . *Irish.* Ah, here—symbols for trees! Oak, Heather, Aspen, and Elder run deep in the heart of the culture.

Like Alice, having innocently followed the white rabbit down the infamous hole, I engross myself in the presented knowledge on the screen. Clicking every link and following every written word deeper and deeper, my curiosity thrives.

The interwoven circle encompassing the markings on my pendant and the wolf's image on the back are both made from the same never-ending knotwork in much of Ireland's ancient artistry.

The part about some symbols and patterns referencing eternity or eternal life is particularly interesting.

One of the links takes me to a photo gallery. Three-quarters of the way down the page, I find a picture of a pendant. So similar to mine, they could be one and the same if only the engravings matched up. The captions below read, *"Over 1,000 years old."*

Could mine be too?

They resemble each other too much to ignore the possibility. But how did it end up thousands of miles away on the tip of a secluded Montana mountaintop? Even more so, if it is, in fact, real, then who in their right mind would wear such a valuable keepsake and risk losing it?

Aware of the hour, I grab my purse off the couch cushion next to me and close the front door tightly behind me as I head out.

It won't take long to get to the restaurant, but that can be said for just about any place in town.

The aroma of charbroiled meat and greasy fries drifts in the air as I open the restaurant door. Two girls sitting side-by-side at a table by the door look up at me as I step inside. Then they quickly look away, giggling and whispering to each other as they watch two guys sitting four booths away along the wall.

After a quick scan of the restaurant for Jamie and having no luck finding her, I walk to the table by the window with the reversed big red vinyl lettering reading *"Celie's Burgers and Fries"* and sit down. My mind wanders as I stare out the window. Cars pass as people step in and out of the shops along the street.

Like at the Glade, memories flood my mind so much that I lose track of time.

A tourist had mentioned to me once that visiting our little town was like stepping into the pages of history—Billy the Kid, sure to show up and raise hell at a moment's notice.

"H E L L O, earth to Shae. You awake in there?" Jamie asks, waving her hand in front of my face. I laugh and shoo it away like a troublesome gnat while she sits down. "Uh, I've missed you," she adds, leaning over and giving me a tight hug.

"Missed you too!" I add, grimacing as she squeezes a bit tighter before letting go.

When she sits back, she has a disapproving frown on her face. "Shae, what on earth are you wearing?"

I chuckle softly. "Well, see, Jamie, this is what we simple folk like to call a shirt," I scoff and give mine a nice tug. "And this? This is a pair of shorts."

"Ha, ha, very funny. I'm completely serious right now. This is you trying? I mean, come on, those aren't clothes—they're a cry for help!"

I smile the sting away. "They aren't that bad."

"Uh, plain! Pink. Ew." She gawks at me.

"I just so happen to like this shirt," I say, grinning with pride. "It's comfy."

"Man, I thought rock bottom was long gone," she says with more intent.

Her concern cracks my conviction, and I shift in my chair, my smile sagging.

"Sorry, I didn't mean—" She frowns and lowers her eyes as she strokes her gorgeous, long, blond hair in a messy braid running down her shoulder. "It's just that when you said you were doing better, I believed you."

Her blue eyes are full of worry when she looks at me again. "But seeing you like this—it's so obvious you're not."

Fidgeting with the silverware wrapped in a napkin in front of me, I shrug my shoulders, unsure how to reply. Like a sister, she holds my best

32

interest at heart, and I love her for it, but sometimes her quick tongue cuts deep—even if she may be right.

"Come on, Shae, talk to me," she says, putting her hand on mine.

I take a deep breath and let it out. "I am trying, you know, to be me again. But it's just so—"

"I know, and I'm sorry I said it like that. I care, you know, and I want you to be fine, but—" She points to all of me. "This doesn't seem like you are. Did something happen after we talked? Was it because I mentioned working with Lainey again that you missed the meeting with her? Too much happening too soon, maybe?"

"You heard about that, did ya?" I force a warm smile.

"I mean, weren't you working there when you met—"

"Yeah." I snarl at the almost mention of the apparently unmentionable culprit. "But I knew Lainey long before any of that. It's just—"

I can't finish my thought. I want Jamie to believe I'm doing better, but the truth is I'm not quite there yet, and I wonder if I ever will be.

I glance at Jamie's super-skinny, hole-ridden jeans and a tight baby-blue tank top that accentuates her chest and brings out her eyes, and I realize I really have stopped trying.

"You know, you're right; I should probably try a little harder." I smile big, hoping to convince her I intend to do as I say.

"I didn't mean to make you feel bad. But you're just so scary to look at right now; I couldn't not say something," Jamie adds with a teasing grin.

"Hah, thanks so much!" I say with a huffy laugh.

"See! A smile. I like that. I just want you to start having fun again."

"I know," I say, grinning as I lean back in my chair. "And I will."

She mirrors my smile, yet it contains ominous undertones as it expands to the point her cheeks crowd her eyes.

"Jamie, no! No way, I know that look."

She shifts her features, calm and collected again. "What? Since we were already talking about having fun, I was just going to suggest going to Duke's tonight. You know, get ready together like old times!"

"I don't know." I narrow my eyes playfully. "I'm not sure I'm ready for what you call fun."

With a toss of her head back, she laughs. "Come on, I'm not that out of control. But look, I promise, no wild outfits. No crazy behavior. Just you, me, and a good time."

I tentatively raise an eyebrow.

"Shae, seriously, you need this!"

Rolling my eyes, I laugh lightly. "Fine, but I don't think this will solve my problems."

"Trust me." She winks. "I got you." And as her cheeks double in size for her evident triumph, she picks up her menu.

We take a few minutes to peruse the food options, even though we've been here over a thousand times and always seem to get the same thing. Soon after we set the menus down, our tall, lanky server, Judy, comes to take our order.

"Well, by golly, Shae, don't you look a sight for sore eyes? Your mom said you was back in town, and I just knew I'd be seeing you two in here!" She winks at me, and I grin.

Out of the corner of my eye, I see Jamie snicker.

Giving her a good kick under the table, I say, "Yep, back again," with a broad, fake smile at Judy. If there was a head of the town gossip, she would be it.

"Your hunk of a fiancé, come with you this time?" Judy asks excitedly, looking out the window.

Gulping down the feeling of angst rising in my

35

throat, I manage to say without a shaky voice, "No. No, not this time." Then I glance wearily at Jamie.

Watching, she smiles warmly and then looks at Judy. "Yeah, on the account, they split up."

Judy gasps. "Oh goodness, no! You poor thing. Did somethin' happen?" Then, trying to suppress what I assume is a smile of intrigue, she covers her lips with the notepad in hand.

"Just a case of irreconcilable differences," Jamie says finitely.

Lowering the notepad from her face, Judy reveals a disappointed grimace caused by knowing she won't get any more details from us, no doubt.

"So sorry, darlin'. That is just sad news indeed. But I bet your mum's happy you're home?"

I nod.

"Good . . . good, so the usual?"

"Yep," Jamie and I both chirp.

Judy leaves, returning a minute later with our drinks, then gives me a sweet smile before heading off again, most likely to spread the juicy news.

"You know she'll go straight to her friends with that, don't you?" I say, disheartened.

"That's the point! Now she won't keep prodding for details, and she still gets to spread her gossipy cheer." Jamie laughs.

"Yeah, but now everyone will know."

"So? The fact is, you aren't engaged anymore. To everyone else, it'll be business as usual."

"Guess you're right," I sigh. "Thanks for that!"

"Meh," she waves her hand dismissively.

She undercuts her thoughtful effort, but her quick thinking has saved me from having to skirt around his absence like the plague for weeks.

Afterward, Jamie fills the void with talk of school and how her parents, who now live in Nebraska, decided to officially cut her off financially, including tuition payments, for who knows how long. I agree; too many C's and D's will do that. It has forced her to quit school and work at the flower shop until further notice. It was only supposed to be for the summer.

"You think you'll still meet up with Lainey, then?" Jamie asks.

"Already called her. A nephew showed up yesterday looking for work, and she gave him the job. It's all right, though; it leaves more time to spend with you." I grin.

"You'll have to find something to keep busy, though."

I nod, not having the slightest idea what it would be.

37

"Look at us—pathetic 21-year-olds with three years of college between the two of us, empty wallets, well, me at least, and nothing good happening since graduation." She snarls and takes a sip from her drink. "Hey, maybe you could get a job at the Grocery Depot," she adds with a hard laugh and a snort at the end.

I cringe. "I'll keep looking, thanks."

"Hey, just trying to help a sister out," she says, then takes a drink as she looks out the window.

"So, you mean to tell me you haven't been doing anything fun since you've been here? Nothin' at all?" I grin, knowing that's not possible in the least.

She cocks her head sharply toward me. As the evil grin forms on her lips, I can't help but laugh.

"Another one, Jamie, already?"

"Two words, Finn Brannon!" she swoons. "He's the dreamiest. Tall. Covered in never-ending muscles. And his hair does the spiky thing that drives me crazy!"

"And why, pray tell, am I only hearing about him now?" I josh.

Jamie looks down and fiddles with the straw in her cup.

"Jamie, I'm kidding."

"No, I know." When she looks up at me, sadness

38

shimmers in her eyes. "It's just, I figured you weren't ready to hear about those kinds of things."

I give pause, my heart sinking. How self-centered had I become, trapped in my own life of misery that my best friend felt she couldn't talk to me?

"Jamie, of course, I want to hear about him—about all of it."

She lets a small grin show on her face. "He's younger than me. Like twenty or something."

I scoff, "That's hardly young. What, like less than six months difference?"

She scrunches her nose at me, as if what I said was unpleasant.

"Anyway, he and his three brothers showed up a few months ago." She grins wide. "Picture Chris Hemsworth as Thor, except with darker hair. All but the youngest, though; he's still in high school."

"Ooh! That *is* impressive," I say breathlessly, imagining such a sight. "So, you guys are dating then?"

Her lips form into a pouty frown.

"Hold up! You mean little Miss *'I can get any guy I want'* hasn't gotten some beau to fall head over heels for her yet? You lose your mojo or something?" I snicker.

With a flick of her braid over her shoulder, she gives a snarky scowl. "Hardly. It's because every idiotic girl in town started freaking out about them! But, of course, by then, I was just another face."

"First, you're never *just* a face, Jamie. And second, he'd be an idiot not to like you."

"No, Shae, like, *all of them!*" she says with widened eyes. "Available or not—young, old, and golden oldies acting like complete morons. I can't be associated with that kind of gobbledygook."

Her dramatics make me laugh. "So, what changed?"

"He looked right past them all." Her eyes twinkle as she looks at me and then down, appearing almost sad. "Finn's different. He treats me like a person, you know. Not just because of the way I look." Then she looks at me again and shrugs. "And his brothers are pretty cool, too. We sometimes all hang out together."

"Okay, I get it. Cool brothers. Cool guy. Then why no date?"

"I don't know," she grumbles. "We talk all the time, and I want to, but he's either working, or I always run into him while he's with his brothers. At first, I was like, *'yeah, all right, this could be cool, I guess,'* but now it's kind of getting on my nerves. It's like they are *always* around," she says through gritted teeth. "Seriously, though, if he doesn't make something happen, I'll do it myself!" Slamming her fist on the table, she makes the silverware and water glasses clank together.

We erupt into cackling laughter; her ultimatum is totally ridiculous.

Our giggling hysteria subsides just as Judy brings us our food.

A large plate with a shiny, greasy bun resting above a bed of lettuce, tomato, onion, pickles, and orange-colored Celie's secret sauce is placed in front of me. Steam emerges from the charred burger, sending the scent of seasoned meat into my nose. Breathing it in makes my mouth water and ignites my appetite once again. French fries enough to feed an army take up over half the plate. I take a big bite of the burger, allowing the rush of memories to wash over my taste buds—juicy and delicious, just how I remember it. The sauce squishes out the sides and all over my hands, but it's worth it.

Jamie finishes her bite of chicken sandwich and wipes her messy hands on a napkin. "Hey, can I ask you something?"

I nod, having just taken a big bite of burger.

41

"Do you think you'll date again? I mean, I know you will, but anytime soon?"

I try to force my food down; it is suddenly drier than dirt.

"I knew you'd bring it up eventually," I mumble out of the corner of my food-filled mouth.

"It's been long enough," she says cautiously.

I take a moment to swallow. "Technically, but I'm just not sure I'm ready."

"Shae, it's not like someone died or anything."

"I know that," I say, a little irked, "and I never said I wouldn't."

She looks at me hard, eyeing my honesty.

"Fine, but I give fair warning. When Finn finally asks me out, eventually, I'll want to double with my bestie, so you better be ready!" she says, adding a knowing grin.

Giving a gentle squeeze to her wrist, I smile. "And if it happens, I'll think about it." And I drink.

"Hey!" she screeches.

"Sorry, when. When it happens," I say, smiling big.

"Ooh, maybe we could get one of Finn's brothers to go with," she says more to herself. "Oh, oh, I almost forgot the juiciest part! One of Finn's brothers dated Maggie. Can you imagine?"

Practically spewing soda out my nose, I cough, "You're kidding?"

She nods enthusiastically. "Supposedly, he broke it off, but she keeps telling everyone they're still together. I haven't confirmed it with him, so I can't know, but it sounds like something Maggie would do."

"She's the worst," I say, wiping my face and the liquid on the table before popping a fry into my mouth.

"Remember when my dad had me in the dunk tank at the festival, and she convinced the baseball team to use me as target practice? I almost drowned."

"Or the rumor she spread about me sleeping with scuzzy Dave?" Jamie says with a snarl. "Had his gross friends eyeballing me for weeks. I could've killed her for that!"

"Man, she tortured us, a lot!" I grimace. "So, when do I get to meet this new guy?"

"Tonight, I hope. They should be there."

Jamie's phone rings loudly, startling us both and making diners shoot annoyed glares in our direction.

"It's Marge!" she whispers as she answers it. The person on the other end speaks fast, their voice loud and angry.

I munch on my food, trying not to eavesdrop, while Jamie eats and listens simultaneously. Every few minutes, she rolls her eyes and says *"yes"* and *"I know"* in response to her boss on the other end.

When she finally hangs up, she sighs long while placing her phone in her back pocket. "New vendors messed up again. Marge is super pissed. I should probably head back."

"No worries, Mom and Dad are back from Twin Falls anyway. Should probably go say hi."

"You going to the 4th of July thing?" she asks.

"Thinking about it. Can you go?"

"Work. But fireworks after, okay?"

I nod with forced enthusiasm while she pulls out two bills from her pocket and sticks them between the salt and pepper shakers.

"See you tonight!" she says then turns and walks to the counter, pays for her lunch, then leaves out the door. On her way past the window, she waves at me again. I respond with a goofy face. She laughs.

When she turns the corner and is gone, I slump in the chair, take another drink, and try to prepare myself for a visit with the parents.

CHAPTER 3

GORGEOUS DISTRACTION

My childhood home is where my parents still live. The same trees I had spent hours playing under have grown ever taller, now a green canopy of memories, ready to greet me when I walk through the gate and up to the open garage.

Dad is busy unpacking the RV but gives a quick wave and says, *"Hey, Pumpkin,"* as he hauls a big handful of stuff into the house.

Mom hugs me tight and tells me how glad she is to have me back.

Then, within the same breath, she dives into the good news about their friend's daughter's recent nuptials to a doctor, surgeon, or whatever his profession is. Of course, what he does for a living is hardly the point, but rather the woman, and how she's my age and married already, is.

Mom's always been a hopeless romantic, marrying my father the day after graduation. They say it has been the most exciting, happy life. I know she wants it for me, too, and thinks marrying me off early will do the trick. Her philosophy—*every second counts.*

And yet she would much rather act like it never happened than acknowledge that I was, in fact, engaged to Jared and almost married if all had gone as planned.

She starts laying into Jared again—a womanizing, good-for-nothing rich kid with everything handed to him by his mommy and daddy and has no values whatsoever. Interesting; she has no problem remembering that bit of it.

For the most part, Mom is sweet and kind and leaves well enough alone when voicing her opinions on others' lives, but when an injustice has occurred to someone she loves, it's no holds barred for that woman.

"Don't get me wrong; he was a *very* charming boy—a little too charming if you ask me. Definitely trying to overcompensate for something." She winks. "If you know what I mean."

"Mom! Yes, we all know you hated him."

"Shae, that's a bit harsh. And you know I never use that word, but severely disliked would be accurate. Who would blame me? So shifty, and, well, you know your father and I never really trusted him much." She looks at me with an *I feel so sorry for you, but I warned you this would happen'* face. "Oh, honey, aren't you relieved you found out who he really was before it was too late and, heaven forbid, children had gotten involved?"

I nod and let her squeeze me into a pity hug.

"And look at you now! Free to get out there and make a life for yourself—no one standing in your way. And the best part—" She squeezes me harder, squishing the sides of our faces together. "You're back here with us, where you belong! And with oodles of suitable men to date. Nope, there's no stopping you now."

From the hint of sweetness on her breath and the uncharacteristically unfiltered advice about a nonexistent dating pool around here, I'd say happy hour had started a bit early. The ride home must have been a lot bumpier than implied.

"Your trip go all right, Mom?"

Releasing me, she rolls her eyes dramatically. "You know your father. Packs in a frenzy, only to race through knee-deep traffic while yelling at everyone and everything for slowing him down just to say he made it home in record time. Yay!" She gives a sarcastic fist punch in the air. "And that's another thing," she adds louder. "With me to help filter out the duds, you'll have no problem finding the right guy. Just you watch!"

Needing to stifle an eye roll, I shrug and smile as I look away, only to see my dog Tax, the cutest yet very old black and white Siberian husky, come around the corner of the garage. He hops up, putting his big front paws on my legs while his tail wags spastically. As I rub his velvety black ears wildly, I hear Mom saying more tidbits of intoxicated wisdom. I only half listen. I know she loves me and cares, but at this point, I can't hear another word of unsolicited dating advice, especially with her altered state of mind. Besides, suppose I were to give even the slightest indication of interest. In that case, she'd have a handful of eligible bachelor *"winners"* lined up to meet me by morning. Her choices, mind you, not mine.

"Well, I better head out, I guess. Let you guys finish unpacking," I say, taking a step back.

"Oh," she says with a slight frown. "If you have to."

"Hey, you think you could check for flyers in the shops for me?" Dad calls, sticking his head out of the garage? "They should all be up, but just to be safe."

"Yeah, no problem." I smile.

"Extras are in the kitchen."

Giving a wave, I go inside, grab the papers, and head back out.

As predicted, when I reach the first block of businesses, which only consists of the Grocery Depot and an antique shop toward the end of town, I can see flyers in their windows. The second and third blocks up are blanketed as well.

The candy store on Main Street emits the scrumptiously sweet scent of store-made boysenberry saltwater taffy every second of every day. It takes over my senses, making my mouth salivate. With depleting willpower, I glance at the window as I hurry past, then continue to the town's two museums while checking all the other shops along the way. Yep, flyers are all there too.

Moving around the corner and up to the library's front doors, I spot more flyers on either side of the double doors.

The heaviness of defeat comes over me. But at least we know my father's employees follow through with directions in his absences.

Taking a moment, I peer in the window at the new book display up front. Several unfamiliar covers rest upright in plain view. The pull to go inside and take a peek tugs at me. Though tempted, I decline, for now.

Eager to get things over with, I move on to the last stop—the Quickie Stop gas station on the furthest corner of town. The syrup in the soda machines comes out thick, and its flavorful goodness is a way better way to end my otherwise unproductive stroll through town.

I walk through the empty parking lot to the station's front doors. As I reach for the handle, the door flings open, almost hitting me in the face. I stumble back, the papers in my hands flying into the air.

"Dang it, I'm sorry!" a tall, scrawny boy, maybe sixteen or seventeen years old with messy dark brown hair and a thin face, says as he twists to reach the papers tumbling on the ground toward him.

"Perfect!" I mumble as a big gust of wind takes several papers into the air. I scramble to catch a few trapped against the garbage can to my left.

Seeing the boy's pitiful, sad face, I quickly feel guilty. "It's all right," I say to him while straining to reach another page. "They're a lost cause anyway." Then I nudge my head at the matching paper in the station window.

"Wow, a festival! It any good?"

"One of the best around." I grin as I right myself.

Reaching out, he hands me his stack of papers. "Name's Niall." Then he goes to grab more off the ground.

"Shae," I reply, organizing what's in my hands.

The door to the station opens again, and I hurry out of the way. Two guys, looking in their twenties, come out laughing, then stop in front of Niall and me.

"Well, *hello* there!" one says as he whisks his thin fingers through his shaggy beach blond hair, exposing his slender face and bright blue eyes full of intrigue.

He's confident in that cocky, *'I'll flirt with anything that moves, but it's all good because I'm hot and can get away with it'* kind of way.

I give a hesitant smile, to which he counters with a grin of his own, proving my point directly.

51

The guy next to him smiles too. I can't help but notice his buff chest, arms, and shoulders are a bit of a contrast to his soft midsection.

"What do you want?" Niall sneers at them.

The blonde raises an eyebrow to a point as a grin forms across his face. "Oh, nothing."

"Knock it off, Sam. Look what your stupid teasing made me do." Niall scowls, thrusting flyers in the guy's face.

Laughing, the guy shoves Niall's arm away. "Not my fault you're lame at flirting!"

A slight twinge of embarrassment sends a rush of heat to my cheeks.

Niall grits his teeth. "Shut up!"

"Niall, grow up!" Sam adds with a hard laugh, then shoots me a flirty wink as he nudges his friend. "Let's go." Then he turns and walks away.

Not following Sam, his friend asks Niall, "You coming?"

"Finn, for the love of all nerds, who cares? Just let Marcas drag him along," Sam calls back, several paces away.

I swallow hard. *Finn*? What are the odds of it not being Jamie's crush?

I look at him again, and he shrugs at us before walking toward the end of the building. When he catches up with Sam, they high-five and start laughing again.

"Jerk!" Niall mumbles, glaring.

I am about to agree with him when the station doors open again. A tall man steps through the doorway and out into the bright afternoon sun from under the overhang. His muscular stature casts widened shadows on the ground at my feet. Striding fingers through tousled coal-black hair, he exposes flawless tan skin, a chiseled jawline, and vibrant evergreen eyes, glistening like rubies in the light of day. Rimmed by dark eyelashes, they are even more mesmerizing to look at.

The words *"Dark-haired Thor"* lodge in my throat, and I desperately try to swallow them back down.

A feeling of desire to be near him smacks me right in the face, and I can't seem to catch my breath.

Casually, he glances around.

When his sights fall on Niall and then me, we lock eyes.

Wildly beating, my heart feels like it will pound right out of my chest if I don't get it to stop. The pull to be near the man magnifies tenfold.

I smile at him warmly. It's a pathetic, simple

thing to do, but I can't control my mouth.

A look of suspicion with a hint of curiosity dances in his eyes as he stares back at me. It sends a rush of electrifying warmth through me, making my cheeks flush red as wild flutters attack my stomach.

The pendant tucked away under my shirt warms like flames against my skin. As I go to rub it, the disheveled flyers slip from my arms, scattering all over the ground.

The man looks down at them, then back at me. His eyes, rich with curiosity, narrow into a guarded stare; his jaw clenched so tight that large muscular bumps appear at the base of his cheekbones.

Every single girl—obsessed!' echoes in my brain in Jamie's voice, and I cringe. He thinks I dropped the papers on purpose.

"Niall, enough playing around; let's go," he calls with a deep, smooth voice while simultaneously putting his sunglasses on. He then turns and walks away, like I no longer exist.

A dull ache replaces the flutters in my stomach. I suddenly feel ill.

Niall reaches down and grabs the papers for me.

"Friendly, isn't he?" I say, taking them from him automatically, too consumed with the mysterious stranger walking down the street to do anything else.

"Who, Marcas? Huh, yeah, I guess not today," he chuckles. "He's my big brother. Those others, too."

Marcas—is that Italian? I shake away the pointless thought. And like circulation traveling back into a numb hand, the spell he somehow cast on me diminishes, forcing me back to my senses.

Marcas—he's not even that cute. "They all that nice?" I ask with thick cynicism as I look at Niall again and give a grimace sort of smile.

He huffs. "They think it's funny to pick on me. I'm used to it, though."

I get the feeling it bothers him much more than he cares to admit, but I let it go.

"Hey, you guys live around here, too, right?"

His eyes light up as he nods. "For a few months now. How'd you guess?"

"Word gets around." I grin.

"No kiddin'?" He blushes. "Well, I better go, or else they'll leave me. See you later!"

"I bet you will," I say, waving as he runs down the street.

I watch Niall meet up with the other three as they are about to disappear around a corner of a building. Then I take off for home, my stomach not feeling up for sweets anymore.

As I walk, I think. And the more I think, the more upset I get. In the hordes of my quandary, I have come to realize two crucial things. Number one: I am a moron. A complete and utter spaz for letting Mar—I can't even say his name without feeling involuntary spasms of irrational excitement course through me—for allowing *his* good looks to make me into a fumbling idiot. And number two: Not now, nor ever, do I want to see *him* again! Undeniably, I know how ridiculous the notion is. Town is a few lousy streets and, like, a dozen shops. So, we're bound to run into each other at some point. But I'm desperate to keep it from happening.

Unable to help it, I begin analyzing the theoretical reasons behind my odd behavior and the sudden feelings I seem to have toward an absolute stranger, especially in the current untrusting, heartbroken state, such as I am in.

Understanding what Jamie meant by ogling girls, a hypothesis quickly forms. Somehow, *his* matchless, physical perfection subdues women into a fit of temporary insanity. And like the carnivorous Venus flytrap, his big, green eyes rimmed with miles of long lashes seduce the unsuspecting and

56

trusting women into his well-laid trap. Memorized by his seductive ways, the women are effortlessly manipulated into falling for him, fast and hard. Then *slap*! He smacks them with a dose of glaring rejection, dashing any hope they have of acceptance. Thus, leaving them confused and wholeheartedly infatuated. Repeat the process, and you have a recipe for disaster in the most stalkerish proportions. We're talking *armed men with large shields and battle armor to fight back the mobs of girls* sort of chaos.

Only time and distance from him will clarify whether I survived the encounter with all my wits kept intact.

In actuality, I should blame Jamie for all of this. She tends to exaggerate good looks to perfection, leaving me to divide said good looks by half, and things usually balance out about right. But not this time. If anything, her description undercut reality by about a million percent—at least with *him*, she did—and now, because of my unpreparedness, I feel utterly humiliated.

Recalling his glare, my stomach turns. He thinks I meant to drop the papers. Like I wanted some act of chivalry or something. And yet would it have killed him to just pick them up anyway? No!

Instead, he acts all put out about it. Like what; good looks excuse proper manners now? Besides, why should I care if he seems interested in me? His behavior makes it very clear he's not, so logically, I shouldn't give him a second thought, right? But for some reason, I do—*many* more of them. Which will make for a troublesome problem if they continue.

Back home, I let the steamy, hot shower water flow over me, hoping it burns enough to snap me out of the mental and emotional conundrum I find myself trapped in.

Without meaning to, his gorgeous deep green eyes flash into my mind. Fumbling with the conditioner bottle, it drops from my hand, hits the shampoo and body wash bottles, and clatters loudly, crashing down to the shower floor. Angry with my recurring unintentional obsession with his muscular pectorals, I kick the bottles to the side and rinse my hair.

It's bad enough I had to think about him all the way home, but now I can't even function properly with simple-minded tasks like bathing without spazzing out? Wait 'til I tell Jamie! She will flip. Out.

"Crap!" I grumble aloud, Finn having popped into my head as I stepped out of the shower. "I can't tell Jamie!" She'll want to know what I think of them, and I can't lie to her. I'm horrible at it. And if I so much as mention being upset with *him*, she'll twist it into something way more outrageous than it already seems.

I guess, if anything, I can at least say they aren't what I expected. Or they are, but I wasn't prepared for it to be true.

I have no choice but to hold out hope that they don't show up tonight. Or at least they don't recognize me if they do. Crap—I'm screwed!

Remembering Jamie's tidbit about one of them dating Maggie, I snicker. Had to be Sam.

I shut off the blow dryer and cinch my bathrobe tighter, just in time to hear a knock at the front door. With it open a crack, I peer around it.

"I come bearing gifts." Jamie smiles widely as she holds up a large bag in my face. "Let's do this!" Then, as I grab her arm and pull her in, she adds, "Nice place you got here! It looks like the boxes vomited your stuff all over," she muses as she moves past the piles of odds and ends still on the floor because I have no clue where to put them.

"You're one to talk; I've been to your place, remember!" I joke from the bedroom doorway. She follows me through.

"Wha-hey, I cleaned it the other day." She scoffs, hands me the bag, and then sits on the bed.

The first outfit, a tight, see-through top, and a skimpy black leather mini skirt, would hardly look good on me, so I sneak it to the bottom of the stack when Jamie isn't looking. The next outfit, a cream-colored, lacy, knee-length dress with a wide brown leather belt and cute cowgirl boots to match, seems more my style.

Standing in front of the full-length, wall-mounted mirror, I see how well the flowing lace fabric hugs my curves, accentuating my hips. How the dipping neckline exposes my slender collarbone and shoulders. Hardly anything of hers ever fits, but though it's a little short, it fits nicely.

"Wow, Shae, you look incredible! I love this on you."

"You do?" I say, turning slowly in a circle. "You don't think it's too much?"

She shakes her head enthusiastically. "And you should do your hair up. It elongates your slender neck." Fidgeting with my hair, she scrunches it up in a messy ball on my head and twists an elastic band into place. Then, pulling down long hairs by my ears, she curls them with her finger. "See? Perfect!"

As Jamie dresses, I admire myself in the mirror for a minute longer, then step away to let her use it.

Up to the mirror, Jamie shifts her body from side to side. The tight black leggings she wears hug her backside. Along with a scarlet shirt—one arm covered to the wrist, while the other shoulder and arm remain exposed—together make her appear a model stepping from the pages of a fashion magazine. Add matching faux-stiletto heels that give her height, seeming even taller than me, and you have every guy's fantasy manifested in the flesh.

We both add our last looks—lip-gloss, earrings, perfume, and my new necklace tucked discreetly under the neckline of my outfit, only the chain showing. Then we head out.

CHAPTER 4

THINGS THAT COMPLICATE

At the edge of town, Duke's is packed, but Jamie gets lucky and finds a parking spot near the entrance. Rows of cars fill the parking lot, crammed so close together I have to squeeze to get out of the vehicle. It isn't unusual to see so many people, though. The campground and summer cabins around the nearby lake keep this place bumping all summer.

The quiet thumping of the band can be heard even outside. But as we step inside the building, the loud drums and heavy base booming intensify, making it difficult to hear much else.

"I hope Finn's here," Jamie yells, the music getting louder the further in the room we go. The glowing white, red, green, and blue lights overhead strobe back and forth across our faces from the dance floor. "He said they would be. I can't wait for you to meet him."

I give a forced smile. Then, having no clue what to do if any of them recognize me, I take a deep breath and prepare for an unpredictable night.

We travel around a group of guys playing pool and up to the bar for drinks. I recognize the bartender at once. Trent has been friends with Jamie and me since junior year, when he moved here from one of the Carolinas; I can never remember which one.

He flips his chin-length, wavy black hair out of his face while wiping peanut dust from the countertop. A barbed-wire tattoo winding around his bicep and a dime-sized gauge in his ear have been added since I saw him more than a year ago. More tattoos travel up his arms but are obscured by his sleeves, making them indiscernible.

He glances at me—his smile wide—and moves to walk over. Stopped by someone stepping up to the bar to order, he puts a finger up for me to hold on a sec. I smile and nod.

Several people from high school, a few years younger than me, sit a couple of stools away. Not knowing them, I don't say hello.

Past them stands a tall, attractive man with satin, russet-colored hair and intense brown eyes. He picks up his glass, turns to face the room, and rests his elbows on the edge of the counter behind him. When he looks in my direction, our eyes connect. A grin forms at the corner of his lips.

My cheeks redden. I smile out of politeness, but my insides scream for him to divert his interest elsewhere.

He steps toward me, taking a drink from the glass as he moves.

My pulse quickens—my heart beating frantically—as he comes closer. Sweat forms on my palms as dread clutches me in its tight grip.

Please don't come over! Please—

"Shae Donnelly," Trent says, leaning on the countertop to my right, his ear-to-ear, dimpled smile being the knight on a white horse to rescue me. "Didn't think I'd see you here any time soon!"

"Trent, wow, it's so good to see you. You work here now?" I say with enthusiasm. Leaning in close, I appear entirely engrossed in the conversation, hoping the other guy loses interest. It works. He stops mid-stride and diverts to a blonde girl who just walked up to the counter.

"Yep, for almost a year now," Trent says, moving around the counter. "You look incredible, by the way." He smiles like he means it.

My cheeks redden as I hug him.

"Hey, listen, I wanted to say that I am sorry. I heard what happened in Seattle," he whispers in my ear, then steps back, his hands clasping my forearms. Then, gazing at me with kind, gentle blue eyes, he adds, "How are you holding up?"

"I'm all right. One day at a time, you know," I say, suppressing the desire to find my mother and strangle her. As much as I pleaded and begged her not to say anything to anyone, I should have known she'd tell her best friend—i.e., Trent's mom. But, thank heavens, the woman has a mouth like a steel trap. Trent takes after her in that regard, thankfully.

Smiling the discomfort away, I hope it's enough to stop further inquiries. Luckily, a quick tap on my shoulder from behind saves me from having to find out.

"I'll find us a table," Jamie yells, then smiles and says, "Hey, Trent," before turning and walking toward the stage.

He mumbles, "Hey," back. "Guess I better get

back." He shrugs shyly. "But we should catch up sometime."

I smile. "Definitely."

Back on the other side of the counter, Trent asks, "You want anything? It's on me," as he fills a glass with beer and then sets it on a tray on the counter.

"Surprise me." I grin.

He pours and adds until the glass is full of a red liquid, then drops a cherry into it. When he hands it to me, I say *"thank you"* and wave bye. He winks and goes about making more drinks.

Out of curiosity, I sneak a peek down the bar at the tall stranger from before. Still talking to a short blonde girl, he sips from his drink as she places her hand on his arm. On her tippy toes, she moves in close, whispering something in his ear. They both laugh. She twirls her hair through her fingers, and he places his hand on her hip, keeping her steady.

Like a train wreck, I can't stop staring. Out of boredom or the grotesqueness of it, I don't really know. Pulling the girl close, he looks down, leaning in for the kiss. Then, at the last second, he turns his head and gives me a wide, seductive grin. My cheeks rush with blood as I scurry away.

Through the crowd, I find Jamie at a table by

the wall. A guy, wearing a warped white cowboy hat looking like someone sat on it, is leaning in close to her. His long, curly mullet coils like crispy tentacles from under the cap.

Just as I reach the table, he stands and speed-walks away like a man on a mission.

"Who was that?" I ask, pulling the chair from the table, then groan when my hand touches something sticky.

Jamie shrugs. "No idea." Then she takes a sip from her drink while scoping the room with her eyes.

"Poor fella. I hope you at least let him down easy?"

"Hey, I can't have him coming back!" she huffs, then snarls at the hard stare of disappointment I give her. "What? He wouldn't take no for an answer." Biting her lower lip in frustration, she points her head to a table a few feet away. "See? None of them will." Two more guys are whispering and staring right at her. "I hope Finn gets here soon," she groans.

My gut tightens at the thought. Will I even get the choice to keep quiet about our previous meeting, or will it be made for me?

Jamie grabs my arm and screeches with delight,

67

pointing spastically across the room. Three familiar-looking, tall men walk through the door. An excited but nervous chill runs through my body out of nowhere. And I instantly scold myself for feeling it.

While Sam and Finn stop at an empty pool table, Marcas heads towards the bar. Moving in quick, fluid strides, each step Marcas takes is light yet purposeful. Watching him, my stomach cramps with more knots. He looks good—unbelievably good.

Ugh, not interested, remember? Besides, based solely on our one nonverbal conversation, his demeanor screams of an arrogant, self-centered, borderline annoyed with the world, better than everyone else jerk. And I am far from being in the market for another one of those.

"He looks so hot tonight, doesn't he?" Jamie gleams as she points in Finn's direction.

"Hardly," I murmur as I scowl at Marcas.

"What?"

"Uh, wait, which one is he again?" I say, narrowing my gaze at the crowd.

"Over by the pool cues. The one with the white and blue striped polo on. Come on," Jamie says, grabbing my wrist and hopping to her feet.

"Wha-hold on!" I resist, giving a slight tug back.

"What's with you?" She pulls harder. "They're here!"

"Yeah, but, since when do you chase?" I state bluntly. Guilt floods me, but I can't go over there. Not just yet.

Her steps stagger to a stop, and she turns to look at me, dropping my arm. "That's not what I'm—" Longingly, she stares at Finn for a second. "I am *not* desperate," she adds, turning back to me.

No, but I am, and I can't stop giving her the sort of half-smile, half-grimace to suggest her actions are contrary to what she may think.

"So, what? I just wait here?" She huffs.

"Maybe? Look, you're kind of hard to miss in that outfit," I say, pointing with my eyes to the table of ogling guys practically drooling. "Go dance, have fun. He'll notice you, trust me."

"You coming?" she asks, her smile resurfacing but not as enthusiastic as before.

"Have to wash my hands," I grimace, pulling my sticky fingers apart, "But you go. Order a drink or something, and talk with Trent."

A wide smirk shines across her face. "Shae, you're a genius! You want anything?"

Holding up my almost-empty glass, I grin and

gulp the last sip before putting it back down.

She goes her way, while I go mine, avoiding the pool table area altogether.

The fluorescent lights above the bathroom sink hum and flicker, the sound of dripping water reverberating off the white-tiled walls. Washing my hands, I stare at my distorted reflection in the bathroom mirror and wonder if the tarnished surface makes me look better or worse. And if it even matters.

Refusing to rejoin Jamie because of where she will ultimately be is stupid; I know that, but I can't help it. Irrational as they are, images of earlier at the station play back in my head like a horror movie. The moronic grin I had on my face, my arms fumbling with papers like an idiot, and me watching Marcas, waiting for him to smile back or say hello. But no, not even a nod. All of it haunts me. And ugh, my hideous clothes, what was I thinking?

After one last deep breath, I dry my hands with the paper towel and step out into the dimly lit hall. A slow ballad hums through the speakers mounted on the ceiling halfway down.

"Oof, sorry," I say, my body colliding with a silhouetted figure.

"Oh, wow there, you all right?" the man asks, steadying me. Then, slowly, he moves into the light. A smile of recognition flickers on his face. "Hey, I saw you before, didn't I?"

"Uh, from the bar, right?" I reply, nerves forming in the pit of my stomach.

His smile widens as he nods. "The name's Brad."

"I'm—"

"Shae, right?"

"Uh, yeah. How'd—"

"I asked the bartender." Then, raising his eyebrows, he takes a step toward me. "I was hoping I'd run into you."

Swallowing down the lump in my throat, I laugh. "Well, here I am."

"That you are." He grins wider. "So, listen, you wanna grab a drink upstairs or something?"

Nothing like skipping to the point to make one's palms sweat. Without thinking, I immediately ask, "What about that girl?" and regret it.

He chuckles. "Nah, not really my type." Then he motions to all of me with a smooth movement of his dark, smoldering eyes. "You are definitely *way* more interesting." Using the tip of his cold index finger, he subtly caresses my upper arm.

A chill of unease prickles up the back of my neck. "Actually, I'm pretty boring." I laugh a corny chuckle to hide my uneasiness as I slowly move my arm away. "Anyway, I can't. My friends are kind of waiting for me up there."

"I find that *very* hard to believe." He beams. "That someone as hot as you don't know how to have a bit of fun."

In disbelief, I stare at his smug face. "But yet it's true," I say, adding a contorted smile of irritation. Then, as I sidestep away from him, he shifts with me.

"Come on now, what's the hurry?" Scooting in a little closer, he bites his lower lip seductively with surprisingly white teeth. "I was kind of hoping we could hang out while I'm here for the week. You look like you know your way around this town. Among other things."

My heart pounds violently as I gulp down annoyance and the underlying fear rising inside me. "Can't; I have plans—with my boyfriend." The second the lie leaves my lips, I wish I could take it back; nothing about it sounds natural.

His smirk lingers on his face as if he knows it too.

Subtly glancing over his shoulder toward the

stairs, toward freedom, I breathe heavily. *'Go! Move your damn legs. Get us out of here!'* my mind screams. But I don't listen.

"Hey, no worries here." He chuckles as he puts his hand on my shoulder and gives a little squeeze. "I won't bite."

"My friends, they're waiting." My voice trembles slightly.

"Come on, come with me. Find somewhere more private, and I'll prove you can trust me."

The words *"trust me"* hit like a slap in the face.

Pulling away from his grasp, I glare. "No, thanks." And I shift to get around him. When he repeats the same dance, I exhale forcefully. "Look, Brad, you—"

He rushes at me. The sour odor of alcohol radiating off his breath makes my nose burn. Holding my breath, I step back. The heel of my shoe rubs against a table leg behind me.

The whimsical love song playing through the speakers on the wall shifts to loud drums and electric guitar.

A playfully wicked smile forms on Brad's lips.

Recoiling, I yell, "I said I'm not interested," and shove past him.

He grabs my arm and pushes me against the

brick wall, holding me tight to his chest. His dark brown eyes sink into mine, penetrating me with his heavy stare.

"Brad, stop! What are you—"

"You tried to hide it." He grins cockily. "But I see you. And if hard-to-get is your game, I'm all in." His eyes widen with lust as he grabs my butt.

Smack!

He grips my wrist tightly, my hand stinging from the impact of it across his cheek. Hostility flickers in his wild eyes. With teeth clenched tight, he leans close to my ear, the stench of hard liquor and cheap cologne making my stomach turn.

"Feisty! I like it!" He breathes hard. "We may have more in common than I thought!"

My body trembles in his grasp as I struggle hard to get my arm free. "Stop it! Someone help! Please!" I cry loudly, my throat burning. But my words only get lost in the roaring music. I look down the hall. No one comes.

Something cold and wet travels down my cheek. I hadn't even realized I had started to cry.

"Please, Brad, don't do this!"

"You know, we could have a really good time, you and I," he whispers menacingly, his voice deep.

Through gritted teeth, I growl, "You're a

delusional piece of crap," and try to wriggle from his grip.

He laughs, wedges his solid chest against mine, then sniffs down my neck and collarbone. Close to my ear, his lips caressing my earlobes, he whispers, "Damn, you smell good."

"Back off!" I yell, thrusting my shoulder into the side of his head.

As he pulls my body away from the wall and slams it back, he roars, "Hold still!"

A sharp cry leaves my lips, the force of impact knocking the wind out of me. Wheezing, I bow over in pain. He grips my hair in his fist and pulls me up. His wide sneer grows more ominous as he propels me back against the wall.

A loud bang comes from behind him, and as he lets up on his grip, I tug myself free and run, only to pummel into someone, almost toppling over them.

Looking down at me with panic-filled eyes is Marcas.

Horrified, my mind racing, all I can do is stare wide-eyed back at him.

"Hey! Dude, do you mind?" Brad huffs.

Ignoring him, Marcas hastily draws me close to his chest, protecting me with his embrace, one of his hands resting on the curve of my lower back.

His touch sends a jolt of unexpected attraction through me. Standing this close to him, he's even taller than I had realized.

"Dude!" Brad yells, taking a step toward us. "You're kind of messing up our private party." He stretches out his hand as if to take me from Marcas.

Marcas scowls so fiercely at him that if looks could kill, Brad would be dead already.

"What's your problem, man?" Brad growls, moving up on Marcas.

"You!" Marcas barks, grabbing a chunk of Brad's shirt in his firm grip, then shoves him back.

He stumbles, then laughs as he straightens his shirt. "Really?" He sniffs smugly. "So, whatcha gonna do about it?" With his chest puffed out, he steadies his stance.

Knowing Marcas could tear Brad to shreds if given a chance, I instinctively grip Marcas' arm, hugging it tightly to me as if his life depended on it. As stupid as it sounds after my earlier encounter with him at the station, I still don't want Marcas getting into trouble—not on my account.

Brad huffs and gives a slight chuckle. "Look, man, you got this all wrong. She's down with it, I swear."

Marcas lunges at Brad. "Marcas, no!" I scream,

pulling him back.

Brad flinches back, throwing his hands up to protect his face. But when nothing else happens, he smirks and puffs out his chest again, as if out of fear that Marcas has backed away.

I won't let go of Marcas. His body is so close to mine that I can feel his strength like an iron rod.

Marcas, breathing hard now, tries to step toward Brad, but I hold him back like an anchor. He looks at me. The unspoken message I see in his troubled eyes gently relays for me to let him go. He turns back to Brad and again steps forward. Too scared to let him out of my clutches, I move with him.

"Leave!" he barks in Brad's face with such conviction that Marcas' whole body vibrates.

Brad only smirks and rolls his eyes.

Gritting his teeth and eyes ablaze, Marcas moves another step forward, appearing a foot taller than Brad. "Now!" his voice booms.

They stare hard at each other, hatred building in their eyes.

But when Marcas doesn't back down, the assuredness in Brad's eyes dims slightly. I don't know if Marcas notices, but I sure do. Slowly, he breaks eye contact with Marcas to focus on me.

And as he walks by, he hits shoulders hard with Marcas while flashing me a threatening grin. Icy chills run through me. He's not done with me yet; I just know it.

Putting his arm around me, Marcas maneuvers me out of Brad's reach and swivels us around until we are safe against the wall.

Brad disappears up the stairs.

Alone, Marcas and I breathe heavily, holding each other close. Even though my body is shaking in his arms, it feels safe and oddly familiar to be held by him. The aroma of his cologne, a musky wood fragrance mixed with a hint of pine, empowers my senses as I breathe it in deeply.

The top two buttons of his ebony-colored polo are undone, exposing his tan, muscular chest. It rises and falls with each deep breath he takes. Then, taking in another, he lets it out slowly, his shoulders relaxing and the anger subsiding.

For the second time today, the pendant around my neck kisses my skin with warmth.

He tips my chin up with his hand to look into my eyes. "Are you hurt?"

His forest-green eyes seem to flicker with concern, so full of compassion. Their warmth and kindness surprise me; I can't help but stare into them, like nothing else in the world matters but him and me. Moreover, I can't rationalize away the uncontrollable attraction I feel for him.

With a mind pounding with a thousand thoughts, I finally shake my head and mumble, "No."

Gently, he wipes a single tear from my cheek, then moves a strand of hair out of my face before resting his hand softly on my shoulder. He is about to say something more when a group of laughing girls round the corner from the stairs and interrupt the moment.

Seeing us standing so close together, they go silent.

Marcas hastily releases me and steps back. The chill of indifference rushes in, replacing the warmth his gentle hands had caused. Neither of us says a word as the girls slowly stroll by, eyeing us suspiciously.

They start whispering to each other as they open the door to the restroom and disappear behind it.

Marcas steps further away, his closeness and concern for me diminishing by the second.

"Well, um, I guess I better back up there," he says, pointing to the stairs, then turns and walks away.

Alone with my thoughts, I combat the overwhelming need to cry, to let my feelings jump into overdrive. I can't—I won't let Brad have any sort of effect on me. So instead, I focus on Marcas, on the raw, palpable emotion he showed. I saw it in his eyes, felt it in his touch—heard it in his voice! I sensed his concern for me in every cell of my being! But his sudden frosty departure leaves a massive mound of doubt in my mind. So much, I am sure I will never escape it.

The bathroom door opens, and the flood of girls returns. Quickly hiding my mascara-streaked face as I wipe it clear, I move to the side to let them pass. But they have other plans than to let me slip away without notice.

"Are you and Marcas dating or something?" A girl with long blonde hair says with a scowl. I recognized her from the group of underclassmen I had seen upstairs earlier.

"Excuse me?" I scoff, caught off guard by her bluntness.

"Are you daft or something? She asked you about Marcas?" another one says, putting her hand on her hip.

"We were just talking," I reply, fidgeting with

my pendant, noticing the heat is gone.

The first girl huffs. "That's not what it looked like to us."

"Better pray Mags doesn't find out you were down here in the dark alone, together!" another one adds with her nose scrunched up in disgust. "You, of all people, should know how bad that would be."

"Cunningham?" I question skeptically. Some girls roll their eyes, while others nod with sass. "But why would she—"

"Because he's her boyfriend, duh!" says the same girl who had brought up Maggie. "Everyone knows that!" She sneers.

The girl standing next to her with a nasty snarl on her face points at me. "You got some nerve mackin' on another girl's boyfriend!" She acts like she's about to punch me in the face. Her hand is shaking a little, an obvious tell that she doesn't have the guts to even try.

"Former boyfriend," one of the other girls corrects, her mousy voice almost lost in the music. "Rr—no, they're back together, for sure," she adds hastily in response to the glares from her friends.

"Like I said, not interested," I mumble, irritated at the accusation of me being a cheater. Then, swiveling on my heels, I brush shoulders brazenly

81

with two more girls blocking the bathroom door as I charge my way through.

Once the door shuts, I lock it and collapse against it.

Marcas? Him and Maggie—together? How could he even stand to be in the same room as her, let alone be her boyfriend? I don't know why it bothers me so much, but it does, and the obsession won't stop.

Still leaning against the door, I hear the handle jiggle and feel a thump on the other side as if someone is trying to force the door open. Brad, back to torment me? A cold rush of panic washes over me.

Muffled cackles of a girl on the other side of the door are followed by the name Derick, and my fears lift. Stepping away from the door, the sour taste of bitterness takes over as I wonder where all these people were when I really needed them.

After fixing my hair in the mirror, I listen again at the door—only heavy, mumbled music vibrates my ear. Unbolting the door, I open it and peek out. Still no one.

Making my way down the hall and up the stairs, I force myself to forget Marcas and Maggie and pray I will never run into Brad ever again.

Between the fog and lights of the stage, I spot Jamie leaning against the pool table where Sam and Finn are playing. Sitting on a chair against the wall, Marcas converses with a girl I don't recognize. It is only now that I realize Niall is missing.

Reluctantly, I make my way over to Jamie.

"Where have you been?" she whispers sharply while handing me my drink. I lift my eyebrows and shrug as I take the glass from her. "Come on, I want you to meet everyone." She pulls me forward. "Hey, guys, this is my friend, Shae, I was telling you about—back from Seattle. This is Sam and Finn." She points to each of them.

My hand half raised, I give an awkward wave and smile at them both.

"Hey, how's it going?" Sam says, smiling, then winks as he had done before.

Unsure if it's something he always does or if he's trying to hint at something, my stomach lurches a little.

"Hi!" Finn smiles, recognition flashing in his eyes but showing no other indication we've already met, and I am unbelievably grateful. "It's nice to finally meet you."

"You, too." I smile, even though I'm not sure if it's true.

He turns to the pool table and hits a ball with the pool cue, knocking three into two separate pockets. Then he shoots Jamie a cute, flirty smile.

"He wants to go with us to see the fireworks," she whispers.

I smile wide. "A date?"

She shrugs and speaks out of the corner of her mouth, "I'll take what I can get."

"I'm going for a drink run; anybody want anything?" Sam asks as he flips his blonde hair away from his face.

I shake my head.

"Sure, I'll have whatever you're getting," Jamie says then turns toward me as Sam walks away, her sly smile broadening.

"And over there against the wall is Marcas. Marcas!" She hollers, calling him with her hand cupping her mouth.

Still talking, he turns his head, raises the hand holding his glass in acknowledgment, then turns back to his conversation.

Jamie shrugs off the lackluster encounter and puts her attention back on Finn and his game.

I wish I could do the same, but the sting of Marcas' passiveness toward our meeting stings a little too much.

So, that's how it's going to be?

Watching his interaction with that girl—his attention locked on her—bitterness threatens to take me over. I mean, she hardly seems his type.

Realizing how pathetically possessive I sound, I recoil. Hostility, this irrational feeling of jealousy, is not me! I have no right, no business getting this worked up about someone who isn't even mine. And obviously doesn't care that I'm not theirs.

I have to force myself to look away and not care what they are doing. However, the giggles and seductive touches to his arm lure me back in, making it extremely difficult to do. Impossible even.

Sam returns and hands Jamie her drink. When she takes it, she glances over at me. Seeing me alone, she comes over. "You good? You seem miffed about something."

"Tired," I say, trying to convince myself to push Marcas and his whatever she is out of my mind.

"You're such a cheat!" Sam harasses Finn loudly.

"Pshaw, right. You tell me how that's even possible. I was over there," Finn protests loudly, pointing to where he had been standing before, three feet away from the pool table.

"I don't know; maybe you did it when I was getting your *girlfriend* a drink?" Sam cries out. Grabbing the pool cue, he chases after Finn, who takes off and hides behind Jamie, using her for protection. While Sam tries to jab Finn with his pool cue, Jamie grips my hand, her eyes excited. *'Girlfriend!'* she mouths. I nudge her shoulder with mine, smiling.

Eventually, Sam gives up and walks away, unsatisfied, while Finn wraps his arms around Jamie's shoulders and rests his chin on her head.

Their happiness makes me smile.

Not wanting to appear creepy for watching, I turn away, and without meaning to, I make direct eye contact with Marcas. Still in his spot, he wears a genuinely warm smile.

Flustered, I look away. But the pull to look again has more power over me than my will to resist it. Hesitantly, I take a peek, and my heart sinks deep. His seat is empty.

Was it even real? Had I imagined it, mistaking the look meant for someone else? Or was that gorgeous smile directed at me? It scares me to think just how much I want it to be true.

But something strange is happening here, something with Marcas. And I don't know if I want to figure it out.

My Venus flytrap theory doesn't seem as far-fetched as previously construed.

CHAPTER 5

NOT AS THEY SEEM

The potent smells of sauerkraut and bratwursts fill the small kitchen. The sound of roaring racecar engines blares through from the other room.

Boycotting the crockpot's content, I grab two slices of bread and start making a sandwich: ham, Swiss cheese, and lettuce piled on thick with several thin slices of avocado atop, followed by a handful of chips on the side.

While preparing my food, I stew over the conversation Dad and I had earlier.

Most times, we get along great, but sometimes

he acts like I'm still his helpless teenage daughter, young, naïve, and in need of constant parental supervision. He overanalyzes everything I say or do to the point of delusion, interpreting what he thinks is happening rather than what actually is. It's irritating. But I sort of get that it's not entirely his fault he can't quite relate to the female mind. He comes from a large family of boys.

Besides, I never said I was afraid to live alone; I only asked for Tax to come home with me. After all, he is my dog, and it'd be nice to have a companion to go home to.

Presumptuously, my father had taken my loneliness as uneasiness, saying if I needed my dog for protection, then maybe I should come home and live where I'd be safe. It's a fair assumption. Living by myself has been an adjustment. But as it is, he has it all wrong and will never convince me his option is better than mine.

Carrying my plate into the living room, I plop on the sofa beside my mom. Sitting in a large armchair with needlework in hand, she whisks away a long piece of silver hair that had fallen over her glasses, then goes back to crocheting. The blanket now reaches mid-knee.

She's a natural beauty, even with the crow's feet

around her grayish-blue eyes and age lines dimpling her mouth.

My parents had been adventurous in their younger years, waiting until much later in life to start a family.

They had no way of knowing I would be their only child.

"Tax is your dog. If you want him, take him. Let me worry about your father," she whispers mid-stitch.

Smiling happily at her, I look at Tax resting on the floor next to my dad's recliner. I love him so much.

Dad jerks in his chair and grunts at something on the TV screen across the room, making Tax perk up his head and take notice.

"See that?" Dad points to the screen excitedly. "Now, that's how you do it!" he says to no one in particular.

Finding the commotion nonthreatening, Tax settles his chin back down.

When the program switches to a commercial, Dad sighs heavily, straining to get out of his chair, then heads toward the kitchen.

"Hey, umm, Dad. You need any last-minute help tomorrow?" I ask while reaching for my water on the coffee table in front of me.

He stops and smiles wide. "All set, pumpkin." Then he continues to the kitchen.

One other thing Dad is excellent at? Letting our little tiffs float away like the wind and leaving one to wonder if they had ever even happened.

I sigh, puffing air from my cheeks. *What to do tomorrow*?

"Ooh, that's pretty!" Mom says, stretching over and gently touching the pendant hanging from my neck. She shifts her bifocals to see it better. "Did you get that here in town?"

"Actually, I found it in the woods the other day. Nice, huh?"

"Really?" She beams, pulling it closer and bobbing it up and down in her hand. "It's so unique-looking and surprisingly heavy. And the sapphire is gorgeous! I'd keep it safe if I were you. Could be worth something."

"Nowhere safer than around my neck," I say with a grin.

She lets it fall, then adjusts her glasses to rest on the tip of her nose.

"So, what trouble have you and Jamie been getting into?"

"Loads."

She chuckles.

"We went to Duke's last night."

"Did she meet up with that new man friend of hers?" She looks at me knowingly for half a second before casually flipping the blanket over and starting another row of stitches.

How did she? "Rrh, yeah," I stammer, watching her closely and finding myself oddly thankful for a mother who loves my friends enough to keep in touch with them even after I've gone. That, or Jamie has been the subject of town gossip again.

"Nothing's official yet, but we plan on seeing the fireworks with him if you want to call that a date. But I guess it's more of a group thing since I'll be there," I rant on. "But he seems nice."

"What about you? Find anyone interesting to talk to while you were there."

A chill creeps down my arms as, first, Brad comes to mind, and then Marcas.

Shaking the unease away, I fidget with a broken piece of chip on my plate. "Not really," I lie. "Just the usual people, I guess. Jamie, Trent—"

Marcas, interesting? Hardly. More like annoying, irritating, and unpredictable in that *I'm a big, hot mess of emotions* kind of way. Is he coming or going? Happy to see me or annoyed as all get out?

92

Interested—not in the slightest. Besides, there are too many questions. Too many underlining qualities.

And yet, he is mysterious, intriguing, and easy on the eyes.

I quickly rattle the dreamy thoughts away. The word *frustrating* swiftly fills the void. I smile out of the corner of my mouth as I pop a small chip in it. Could such a word be more accurate? Marcas and me. The idea seems utterly laughable.

"What about one of Finn's brothers? Girls seem to like them," Mom asks, as if she's been reading my mind. "Were they there, too?"

"I don't think I'm their type, Mom," I state flatly.

The idea of swooning over them like every other ridiculous girl in the area makes me snarl internally. And when I realize where my begrudging attitude stems from, I again scold myself for doing what I hate.

"Shae, don't be snooty! You'll never know unless you get out there and see for yourself."

"Hey, I am not a snob! Besides, I think I'm fine where I'm at right now," I say, then stuff the last bite of the sandwich in my mouth.

With a pat on my leg, I call Tax over. He

stretches his legs out in front of his body, yawns widely, then trots over, wagging his long, fluffy tail behind him.

"See, now, when you say it like that, I don't know if I believe you," Mom says. "I only want you to be happy again. That's all."

Recognizing the familiar tone of concern and knowing she's about two seconds away from a full-on mom lecture, I tread lightly. "Well, I kind of am."

"And that's supposed to convince me?" She looks over her glasses, smirking skeptically.

"You already know I need more time, or else I wouldn't have moved back," I say, letting Tax lick my outstretched hand. "But I am glad I did. And Jamie's been a big help, too."

"I know, sweetheart, but I just hope you don't put blinders on to the rest of the world while you figure things out. You might miss the perfect person right there in front of you."

And there it is: her daily pearl of wisdom. She's not wrong; I just don't like being told what I already know.

"Have you been rereading those self-help books?" I grin.

She scrunches her nose at me and playfully

94

swats at my pant leg. "Don't knock them until you try them. They have some good advice to give."

I roll my eyes at her good-humoredly. She laughs and goes back to stitching again.

Tax scratches at my hand and then rubs his face and nose on it.

"You're such a good boy, Tax," I say as he smacks his tail against Mom's leg. I mush his face and give a playful rub on his head. "Whaddya think, Tax? Want to go for a run? Huh—do yuh, huh?" His tail wags wildly.

Mom smiles. "He sure did miss you."

"Me too." I pucker up, kiss him on the head, and then stroke his soft ears. "Anyway, I should probably get going. Kind of have stuff to do—"

"People to see," she finishes with a smirk.

Getting off the couch, I lean over and hug her. "Love you, Mom." Then I go into the hall and grab Tax's leash off the table. "See you guys tomorrow," I call, opening the front door. Neither one looks away from what they are doing, but both wave goodbye.

As I run down the tourist-crowded street, I skirt from side to side to avoid them and signs stuck in the curbside grass advertising the festival. Tax pants alongside me, sniffing at street posts and flowerpots as we run past one of the town's many thrift stores and down a back alley. The air feels cool and refreshing against my skin. With every heavy step I take, it's like I am stomping on a troubling thought, snuffing it from my mind and leaving my worries and stress trailing behind me.

Two other runners, each wearing gigantic headphones, whoosh by and wave. One of them looks familiar, but they are long gone before I even have a chance to take a second look.

I continue past the shops and behind the museums, then turn right onto an alleyway leading through the rest of town. At the end, I go left and sprint to the top of the hill that descends into the far end of the town park. A bright orange, square-holed fence surrounds the grass for tomorrow's car show. I move on through to the field.

The grass is prickly soft under my outstretched legs. Eager to be set free, Tax scratches my hand until I take off the leash and let him play while I rest. Using energy I didn't know he had left, he runs in circles all over the field like a puppy, darting in and out of the trees surrounding the park. Then, barking at something, he runs out of sight.

"Tax, don't go far!" I yell. When he doesn't pop back into view, I whistle. "Here, boy," I call again.

No response.

Walking down the line of pines at the edge of the park's boundary, I find him facing the forest, his large eyes focused on something within the dense bushes.

"There you are. Come on, back to the grass." His ears perk up as he whimpers and begins pacing back and forth. "Tax, what is it?"

A shrubbery branch snaps with a loud *crack*.

I inhale sharply, the sound sending a chill of fright right through me. Tax lowers his head and lets out a grumbled growl.

"Shh, boy, it's okay," I say, grabbing his collar and scanning the trees for movement. The hairs on my arms prickle with unease. I take a timid step forward.

"Whatcha lookin' at?" comes a voice beside me.

Shrieking so forcefully my throat burns, I jump back.

"Niall!" I growl and slap his shoulder with the back of my hand. Feeling like I'd hit bricks, I instantly wince in pain. "Don't scare me like that!"

"Nice vocal range you got there!" he says, trying to suppress a laugh. But when he notices me gasping for breath, he winces. "Sorry, I didn't mean to get you *that* bad."

"Ugh! You sure about that?" I pant.

"What were you looking at anyway?"

"I heard something," I say, pointing to the forest with one hand while clutching my pounding chest with the other. "I couldn't see what it was, though. Try to make a noise or something next time! Geez. And stop laughing!"

"Sorry." He tries to smother another laugh with a hand over his mouth. "But you should have seen your face. Man, you're jumpy!"

"Whatever," I add as I try to stifle a smile of my own. Seeing the fake pout on his face, I shove his shoulder. "Stop that. It's not funny!" I add, forcing my smile to leave. "I mean it. I've had it rough, so cut me some slack, would yuh?"

His smile falls. "Crap, I totally forgot," he says, his tone turning serious. "I'm such an idiot. I wasn't—."

"Wait, forgot what?"

"About last night. Marcas kind of told me."

"What?" I say as a rush of embarrassment blankets me. Then Marcas' frigid behavior comes to mind, and anger shifts inside me. I mean, now he's back to caring? "Wh-why would he even—"

"He thought I was your friend and should know," Niall says, watching me closely.

"Uh, okay," I say, irritated, looking away. "Guess you all know my business now?" I mumble.

"What? No! Shae, no one else, I swear."

Hearing the worry in his voice makes my vexation subside, and I turn around with my arms folded. But when I see the concern in his eyes, I regret my harshness even more.

"Sorry," I sigh, "it just surprised me that he'd bother to even say anything about it. It wasn't that big of a deal."

Niall puts his hand on my shoulder. "That's not what he said."

For a moment, my heart sputters. So, Marcas cares about me, after all? At least enough to tell Niall?

"You sure you're all right?"

I nod and look down at the faded reddish marks on my wrists.

"That guy did this to you?" Niall gasps, grabbing for my arm.

"Niall, I'm fine, really," I say, trying to hide it, but he won't let go.

Looking down at the welts, he then looks up at me, scowling harder. "Now, I'm really glad Marcas showed up. This could have ended really badly, Shae."

I nod in agreement as he lets my arm fall.

"I don't know what all he told you," I say, gesturing for Niall to sit with me under the closest tree. I'm not even sure I want to know or could even handle it even if I did know, but I have to find out. "But afterward—back upstairs. He didn't even bother—I mean, I'd have at least talked with me again—made sure I was all right. Wouldn't you?"

"Well, yeah, I'd like to think so." Niall shrugs. "But maybe he didn't want to embarrass you? Or, you know, maybe he was preoccupied and didn't get the chance."

Yeah, by some girl!

"Suppose so," I say quietly. "Guess it doesn't matter now, does it?" I add with a forced smile.

"But it did," he says somberly. "If it helps, I know he's been struggling with a lot of stuff lately. So, maybe that's why."

"Maybe." I shrug, but the curiosity remains. "Like, what kind of stuff do you think?" I hate asking, but I have to know what would be so distracting that he couldn't find the time to talk.

"Oh, for sure, work! I mean, he literally took over the family business a couple of months ago. Kind of a big deal for us. And I know for a fact he wasn't ready for it. But then again, he didn't have a choice."

"Work," I say placidly. Funny, it didn't seem to hold him back from talking with that girl he couldn't get enough of.

"Yeah, this one job we're doing makes him so frustrated. Can't seem to figure it out."

"'Kay, I guess that would be a distraction."

No, no, I don't see it! Not for a second.

"Or it could be that our parents died and left him responsible for Sam, Finn, and me. The change hasn't been easy for any of us. But I guess either one would do it."

Heavy, judgmental guilt sucker punches me right in the gut.

"Niall! I'm so sorry! I didn't know!"

He chuckles his sadness away. "It's okay; how could you have?"

"How long ago did it happen, your parents, I mean?"

"My mother died quite a few years ago, but my father went at the end of last year."

Full of self-loathing for assuming the worst in Marcas and letting my harsh thoughts get the best of me, I squirm in my seat. I should have known better. I know firsthand how death, grief, and pain can make people act differently than they usually

101

would. Maybe Marcas didn't mean to be so distant and unfriendly toward me, not intentionally anyway.

"That must be hard to move on from," I whisper, having no other words to ease the pain I see in Niall's eyes.

He nods. "But we do, you know? Because we have to, right?"

I smile sorrowfully and nod my head.

With no outward signs that the heart aches on the inside, it's easy to forget that, just like me, others are going through just as much pain, if not more than me. I should try and remember that.

Lost in thought, it takes a second for me to realize Niall had spoken.

"You sure you're okay?" he asks again, watching me knowingly. "Still upset about last night?"

Finding his intuitiveness surprising, I shrug and half-smile. "Yeah, but it's not just that. It's fine, though. You don't have to—"

"Uh, yeah, I do. Now you have to tell me." He smiles big. "I won't let you leave until you do."

His support makes me want to trust him, but I don't know if I have it in me.

"Right. Let me just go ahead and unload a bunch of emotional garbage on you. We only just met. It's totally normal!" I chuckle, being half-serious. No way Niall wants to hear about it.

What would I even say? *'Yeah, sure, my fiancé cheated on me, and that sucks, but hey, it's all good because I have an irrational crush on your brother. I mean, we just met, and I'm pretty sure he finds me revolting beyond all reason as he feels about all the other lame girls in town, but that doesn't mean we can't make it work, right?'*

"If it'll help, why not?" Niall says so earnestly, genuinely, understandingly, and in want of helping that I can't ignore it.

Inhaling deeply, I then let it out. "I give fair warning; it's complicated."

"I'm sure I can keep up." He grins.

With my legs crossed under me, I pick at the grass.

"I guess it started like most love stories: girl meets boy and falls hard. Boy asks the girl to move to the big city, and she blindly accepts. Then, after a couple of years, the boy asks the girl to marry him. But what he doesn't bother to do is let her know he's been seeing someone on the side for damn near the entire time they've been together. So, the girl gets blindsided days before the wedding when the boy goes off to marry the other girl, who turns out to be the girl's old college roommate."

"Wow!" Niall says with a heavy breath. "Dang, that's cold."

"And the seriously messed up part about the whole thing? Stupid girl can't figure out how to move on without stupid boy."

"You're still in love with him, then?"

"No. I mean, how can I be?"

"Dude, right? Selfish jerk!"

"Right! And the trust issues he left me with. It's like, whoa-really? So, now what am I supposed to do?" I shrug away the fresh ache that pains its way into my heart. "More than anything, I feel lost."

He gives an encouraging smile as sadness hides in his eyes. "And coming back and dealing with stuff like last night doesn't make it any easier, does it?"

"Exactly! Starting over is hard enough as it is."

"I'm no expert, but I'm pretty sure things will get easier."

"Some things have, I guess."

"Hey, and let me just clarify here," he says formally. "We're not all pushy, backstabbing, cheating jerks."

"Eh." I smirk. "I guess not," I add when his face scrunches up in horror.

"Hey, listen, don't-don't tell anyone about this, okay? It's embarrassing, and I've tried hard to keep people from finding out about it."

"Don't worry, I won't," he says, looking at me so intently that I wholeheartedly believe him. "Seriously, though, if you need anything—someone to talk to or sit with—I'm here for you, just so you know." He puts his hand gently on mine and gives me a little squeeze.

I smile at him, knowing he isn't making a move but consoling me. In such a short time, he's become quite the confidant, and I am incredibly grateful for him.

"Thanks." Then I nudge his shoulder with mine. "You're a good friend, Niall. I'm glad you ran into me yesterday."

"And today!" We both laugh.

Feeling stiff, I stretch my body while looking again for Tax. I spot him halfway across the field, lying under a tree with his head resting on his crossed legs in front of him.

Marcas and Maggie enter my thoughts, and as much as I would love to shut them out, I can't.

"Um, hey, so I was kind of wondering about somethin'. Is it true, you know, that Marcas dated Maggie?" I say, trying to sound casual, but I'm sure

Niall sees right through it.

Niall snorts. "Ugh! Yes. She a friend of yours?"

"Not even."

"Man, we couldn't stand her either. She kept bringing her two friends around to get Sam and Finn to hook up with them."

I laugh, even though I'm nervous to ask, "Why'd they break up?" My heart is pounding.

"You know how those kinds of girls are. Possessive and stuff. Marcas wasn't serious about it, so it got old quick. And the rest is history. Well, sort of. She keeps coming around, begging for a second chance." He laughs and lets out a little snort. "It's kind of pathetic. Sam and Finn live to give Marcas crap about it. It gets under Marcas' skin *so* bad." He chuckles and then looks more serious. "Why'd you want to know?"

"Eh, girls last night threatened any interest in Marcas would bring on the wrath of Maggie," I say with a level tone as if I don't care either way. Still, I can't help the rage of jealousy igniting inside me. "Like I could ever be afraid of her."

He huffs. "I don't know; she's pretty scary. But I guess you don't have anything to worry about. That is, unless you are interested in Marcas." He grins and pumps his eyebrows up fast twice. "Wouldn't say I blame you; he is quite the guy." Then he laughs.

"*No*! I am definitely *not* interested, thank you." I force a laugh out, but not seeing the same humor in the idea as he does, it sounds a little disingenuous. "I was just checking facts. Not that I care or anything," I say a little too persuasively.

"If you say so." He smiles a playful grin.

Knowing there's no way to recover my dignity on the subject, I casually check the time and realize it is conveniently getting late.

Niall shifts his body and gazes up into the feathery, leaf-filled branches of the tree. "You got to go?"

I nod. "Hey, what are you doing tomorrow?"

"Does sleeping in and eating a whole box of cereal for brunch count as something?" He chuckles.

"The festival's tomorrow. I was thinking of going around ten. You want to come with?"

"Uh, yeah, that sounds awesome, actually!"

"Sweet! Let's meet at the coffee shop on Main, then head up the hill together."

He nods and smiles widely. "I'll be there."

"Bye," I say as I wave, then run to catch up to Tax. I reattach his leash and am about to jog away when I glance back to wave again at Niall, but he's already gone.

CHAPTER 6

WILD, NOT FREE

The cool air caresses my warm cheeks as I leisurely walk along the gravel path on the other side of the road from my cabin. It had been silently persuading me to travel down it since day one. So, since sleep had eluded me yet again, leaving me plenty of time before meeting Niall, I am compelled to take the path up on its offer for adventure. I know it will not disappoint.

It has been years since I have gone this way, giving the morning a new and exciting feel. A gentle, almost mystical stillness takes over when the early morning sliver of light gleams onto the towering, needle-filled evergreens and the striped

Aspen trees spotted among them. The scene's intoxicating pull lures me deeper into the woods.

Tax sure would like this, but mom insisted on taking him to the groomer instead.

As I walk, I caress the pendant around my neck, sliding it back and forth along the chain. The behavior is automatic now—I can't recall what life was like without it.

The strange dream from the other day shifts in my mind. Somewhere deep in my psyche, it begs me to find meaning within all of it. Of course, logically, it was only an obscured side effect from the unfortunate emotional meltdown that occurred moments before finding the necklace and falling asleep. But how can I deny their similarities? The pendant's origin and the woman's accent cannot be coincidental. The notion they are connected somehow is almost unshakeable.

Sweat glistens on my brow. Taking off my jacket, I stuff it in my backpack and continue down the path. It guides me further into the thick forest, the alluring aroma of pine soothing me as I go.

Marcas' face flashes in my head, but I hurriedly stifle the image away, thankfully finding it easier to do.

When I can see the brilliant rays of sunlight

flicker through the trees again, I stop to rest. The faint babbling of a flowing river hides in the background while birds' beating chirps sound in the surrounding trees.

As I sit on a log on the ground encased by a circle of tall trees, I grab a pencil and a sketchbook from my bag. Slowly sifting through the pages, I pass several unfinished renderings, and sadness sets in.

Art is as much a part of my identity as this forest. How could I have let someone keep me from the things I love for so long?

Not anymore—not ever again.

Taking a deep breath, I close my eyes and let the sounds around me bring me back to my center. Then, slowly releasing my breath, I open my eyes and flip through the rest of the book until I reach an empty page. Focusing on the forest before me, I take in the trees—tall, short, thriving with life or bent and broken, corrupted by bug decay, fire, and death; they stretch far out around me. Their jagged, broken branches, dark brown pine needles, and brittle pinecone remnants carpet the earth underfoot, several feet deep.

Touching the pencil lightly to the page, I roughly sketch barbaric lines and shapes for the mountains, heightened trees, and undulating skyline. With every dark, thick pencil stroke I add, more of the forest's tragic story manifests on the page.

Up at eye level, I examine the likeness. Movement, out in the unfocused distance beyond the page, catches my eye. Two enormous wolves approach from the bushes less than fifty yards away.

As if violently ripped from me, the breath in my lungs scrapes as it leaves my throat. I watch two more wolves trot into view and follow alongside the others. Low to the ground, they keep to the taller grass.

As I rush to the nearest tree, the pad and pencil tumble to the ground. I am breathing so frantically that I nearly hyperventilate as I leap high and straddle my thighs and arms tightly around the trunk. Muscles burn with fatigue as I fight with everything in me to lumberjack my way up.

But it is in vain. The tractionless soles of my shoes slip, and I slide, my skin grating on the rough, knotted bark to the ground. Long scarlet-red scratches track down the inside of my arms. They sting like a million knives, cutting my skin as blood beads to the surface. But I don't have time to care.

The wolves are almost to me. Zig-zagging stealthily, they watch me with wide, beastly eyes.

Grabbing the longest stick I can find on the ground, I then lift it to waist level in front of me just as the wolves skid to a stop a yard or so away.

The lone wolf out in front—a giant, horrid creature with shaggy, brownish-gray fur and dark, polarizing, golden eyes that narrow in on me like we are the only creatures for miles—takes a step forward, while the others remain still.

"Hey!" I scream and thrust the stick at it. "Go on—get out of here!"

It doesn't even blink as it takes another step closer.

"I mean it—get out of here!" I stammer, my voice trembling as violently as the stick in my hands.

It takes another step.

"Stop!" Panic bubbles up inside. My legs wobble slightly. Don't—don't you even pass out!

The determined wolf meanders a bit to the right. Fixedly, I follow it with my jittery stick. It moves back, and I do the same. Willing to do this dance all day long, I regrip my weapon tighter.

"Get—*back*!" I yell aggressively and swing the stick at it again.

Hearing a scuffling sound behind me, I slowly turn my head and gasp in horror. The other three wolves now occupy the area beyond my tiny half-circle of trees behind me, having moved into position while I was distracted.

Panting heavily, I twist aggressively in a circle, my stick swinging wildly.

"I mean it—stay away!" I screech so loudly my voice goes hoarse.

Striking a nearby tree, my only protection snaps in half with a gut-wrenching *crack*. I feel the blood drain from my cheeks as one of the pieces falls to the ground. I hurl the broken piece at the alpha and back myself against the only safety I have left—a tree behind me.

The alpha remains statue-like as a sinister, almost human-esque smile of enjoyment spreads across its face.

The wolf wrinkles its nose, the upper lip rising with it. Grotesque, bloodstained fangs, seemingly as sharp as an eagle's talons, gleam at me in the light as it takes another step toward me.

Suddenly, it stops and looks sharply over its shoulder. Headed straight for us with sprinting swiftness are four more wolves.

With its head held high, the wolf in front of me

gives a snarly snort before letting out a thunderous howl, deep and aggressive, seeming to rise from the depths of its belly. Then, without warning, it springs at me.

A blood-curdling scream leaves me as I dive to the left, landing hard on the ground. The birds in the trees above squawk loudly, scattering into the sky. Shrill yelps of pain are heard as the heavy-bodied wolf collides with the tree I had just been standing in front of.

"Please don't let it get back up!" I beg as my heart pounds in my chest. Deep, throbbing jabs of pain shoot up my forearm. Wincing, I clutch my arm to my chest as I watch the alpha get up and shake leaves and forest debris off its back. But it does not look my way.

As if given a silent command, the original three and their leader attack the newcomers with bounding force, their bodies barreling into them with a mighty *thud*.

I stifle a scream into my shoulder. Merely feet from me, monsters sink dagger-sharp teeth into each other, ripping and shredding skin while sending fur flying in a frenzy of madness. It makes my stomach turn; the smell of blood is in the air.

For a moment, I am forgotten as the gruesome

display of predatory war continues all around me.

The overwhelming rumbling of rustling leaves, booming barks, high-pitched yelps of agony, snarling and chomping of clacking teeth, and the aggressively deep growls, almost demonic sounding, sway close to me then away again, coming at me from all sides like the whirling motions of a tilt-a-whirl. I try to block them out, clamping my hands tightly around my ears, but the harrowing sounds find their way through.

With murder in its black eyes, a wolf lunges for me, only to be tackled away at the last second by one of the newcomers.

My heart thumps frantically in my chest. Did that one just save me? But then my stomach lurches. No, not a rescue, a takeover. They very well could be fighting for the rights to my flesh!

The trees and sky warp into a shaky, blurry haze around me. Clenching my eyes tight, I try to will the spinning to stop.

I have to get out of here!

When my eyes open, the alpha wolf immediately comes into focus across the clearing. Watching me through the commotion of battle, it sneers its repulsive teeth at me as it shifts its paws on the needled ground then springs into a sprint, coming right at me with lightning speed.

The scream that erupts from me drowns out all other sounds. Paralyzed by fear, all I focus on is the wolf's evil eyes drilling their hate into me as it charges. There is no way for me to get out of this alive.

Two yards away, then one. Only feet away now. It jumps. I take in a sharp breath. A flash of movement. Seconds before impact, an enormous black-haired wolf skids to a stop before me and hurls the advancing alpha away. Dirt and needles spray across my body. When the dust clears, the other three newcomers are standing guard on all sides of me. Red blotches of blood stain the fur on their legs, shoulders, and faces.

Eyes glowering, locked on me, the brownish-gray alpha growls heavily, sniffs the air, then begins pacing as its pack falls into line behind it.

Standing directly in front of me, my black-haired hero lets out a stiff grumble of warning. I imagine it to mean *'Back down!',* or at least I desperately wish it to be so.

The alpha lunges forward, and I scream. But my hero, anticipating the attack, bites down hard on my attacker's leg. It lets out a high-pitched yelp as it recoils back to its pack, eyes glaring and teeth snarling. My hero barks twice and rumbles a throaty growl that I know means, *'Try that again, and I'll kill you.'*

The alpha sniffs a snorted, angry grunt as it takes a step back, stretches its head to the sky, and lets out a loud, drawn-out, vibrating howl. The eerie sound inundates the forest in a haunting echo.

With its tail curled low, the alpha trods away. Its pack follows, fading back through the trees.

Slowly, the victors turn, facing me with guarded eyes.

My body shakes uncontrollably as teardrops stream down my dirty face. I don't dare wipe them away—to move at all. All I can do is stare wide-eyed at my protectors, unsure if they remain to be.

All is still—except for the rapid beating of my heart in my ears and the unnerving ringing silence crippling me to my core.

The black-haired leader steps up to me. So close to my face, it stares its golden-rimmed green eyes into mine. Fear trembles through me as I wait for the end.

Minutes pass; how many, I do not know, for I find myself lost in a sea of dazzling green, familiarity in the wildness of the animal's eyes I cannot turn away from.

Tepid, delicate puffs of air tickle the hairs around my forehead as the animal sniffs about my head. I inhale sharply, the dog-like scent wafting into my nose.

Then, as if it is the most natural, normal thing to do, the wolf yawns widely as it crouches down and lazily lays almost against my leg.

Slowly, cautiously, I reach my hand out, palm up. "Hey there," I whisper, swallowing hard, my mouth so dry I can hardly accomplish it. "We're all friends here, right?"

Giving a double sniff to my fingers, it lowers its head and softly touches its cold, wet nose to my palm. Bursts of charged energy surge through me like touching an electric fence.

I smile, my breathing heavy and staggered. "See, you're not going to eat me, are you?"

Around me, the other wolves stretch and settle down in the shade of the trees before licking their wounds.

Why? Why did they protect me? I had been theirs for the taking, yet they did not attack, which does not make sense.

I watch the black wolf lick its lips and pant like Tax would.

Overwhelmed by their acceptance of me, I hold back sobs of relief—of thankfulness.

The wolf next to me blinks, licks its black nose, and looks at the others before looking at me again. Rising to its feet, it comes closer to my face and nudges its nose under my chin, resting it there almost as a sign of affection, perhaps respect. Then it prances away, its beautiful fur ruffling in the movement as it follows the others already capering back into the thick of the distant forest.

At the tree's edge, it stops for one last look. In awe, I watch as it lifts its head and howls; the warm, deep, yet underlying sad tones resonate through my soul. It is a sound I will never forget.

Into the bushes, it runs, vanishing from sight.

Feeling heavy, like a bag of rocks, I collapse to the ground and let out a shaky exhalation, sobbing loudly with tears pouring from my eyes.

I am a strong woman, capable of handling most things, but the encounter is almost too much.

Get up! You can do this.

I blubber more and take in a breath.

They didn't hurt you. They left. You're just fine. Now, get up!

My hands tremble, covered in dirt, crumpled leaves, and needles, as I wipe hair off my face and force another sob away by breathing deep, steady. Mimicking the rhythm several more times, soon my palpitating heart slows.

Teeth clenched, I stand up, grab my jacket, tie it like a sling around my arm, fling my bag over my other shoulder, and then take off for home.

Looking in my bathroom mirror, I examine the dirt-streaked trails on my cheeks, chunks of leaves in my hair, and the dark blobs of dried blood on the scratches under my arms.

Pushing back against the waves of panic and fear tugging at me, I try to figure out if I even have it in me to finish the day as planned.

The cold chill of the water I splash on my face is jarring yet soothingly satisfying. I close my eyes and breathe deeply. "I can do this," I say aloud and open my eyes again, looking at my reflection in the mirror. "Forget it even happened."

Though difficult to do because of my arm, I change my clothes and freshen up my face as quickly as possible. Less than an hour remains before I am to meet Niall.

I'm about ninety-nine percent sure my arm isn't broken. But the throbbing pain feels too deep to be maintained by any degree of over-the-counter pain relief, so I head to the clinic next to the hospital ER doors.

A nurse I don't recognize calls me from the waiting room.

Several x-rays later and a long wait in the exam room, I am finally seen by the doctor—the resident "out-of-towner" intern. Having limited patience for trivial trauma such as my hurt arm, he quickly passed me off to a disgruntled nurse who had been about to head home for the day.

"You fell on it?" she questions again as she puts my arm in a black corset-style splint. "This morning?" Her eyes shift, examining the rest of me.

"It was stupid, really. I tripped over my shoelace while hiking," I say, wincing as she tightens the Velcro straps.

"And you're sure it was from the fall *today*?"

"Well, yeah. I mean, why wouldn't it be?"

Her eyes narrow. "You see this greenish bruising here at the wrist? That means it's an old wound, on the mend. Days, possibly a week old. And the scratches? Scabbed over."

How could that be? I almost examine my wounds myself but think better of it.

"You dating anyone, Miss. Donnelly?" she says, jotting something down in my chart.

"No," I say nervously, remembering the marks

on my arm from Brad. I look down at them casually, but they are no longer visible. I smile at her. "Not for a while now."

She eyeballs me as she finishes the rest of my paperwork. "Nonetheless, Miss Donnelly, should your story change, know there are people around who can help." And, though obviously annoyed with me, she smiles warmly for a few seconds before the hard crust of bitterness returns to her face as she looks down again.

She taps the papers to file them into alignment, then puts them in the manila folder on the table before handing me a white slip of paper with a messy, unintelligible signature. "They'll fill it just outside at the pharmacy. You better hurry; they close in a few minutes. Ice your arm often, get plenty of rest, and don't take the splint off except to shower. Here—" She shoves a plastic bag in my hand. "Eat the granola bar in there when you take the first pill. If you still feel discomfort, follow up with your regular practitioner in two weeks." Then she leaves.

Out in the hallway, I check the time on the wall. 10:10 a.m. Late again.

I move up to the tall counter in the corner of the gift shop. The balding, middle-aged, big-boned man behind it recalls my name and prescription without me saying so, as if he had been expecting me. I nod, show my ID, and pay. Upon giving a receipt, and before I even step away, the man flips a *'Closed for the holiday'* sign on the counter. He then quickly pulls the gate down, the loud metal clanking resembling the clatter of a closing prison cell door.

CHAPTER 7

CONFUSION

Niall is only a few short blocks away, but I power stride like it will take an hour to get there.

Leaning against the corner building, Niall faces the steep road leading to the town park. Occupied by people watching, he fails to notice me sneaking up behind him.

"Hey!" I say, rattling his arm.

"Hah, 'bout time you showed," he says, seemingly unfazed by my jarring as he swivels around smiling. "Thought you'd changed your mind!"

"Not a chance!" I say happily.

"Wow, hey, what happened there?" he adds, pointing to my arm. "You okay?"

"Oh, uh, yeah, it's nothing." I smile coyly, maneuvering my splinted arm subtly behind my back.

He frowns. "Doesn't look like nothin'." Reaching over, he removes a small leaf tangled in my hair. "Have you been rolling around on the ground?"

I laugh, "Not exactly." Then I shake my hair, releasing stray leaves I may have missed.

"Guh, a spider landed on you, didn't it, and you freaked?" His body shudders spastically like one is on him right now.

"It was *not* a bug," I say, trying not to laugh.

"All right, then what?"

"Really, Niall, it was nothing," I say more seriously and nudge my head in the direction I desperately wish we'd go. "Come on, let's just go. Everything's already started."

Deep wrinkles line his forehead, and when his eyes stiffen with concern, a heavy weight shifts into my chest. "Please . . . Niall?"

"Shae." He says my name so firmly that my heart sinks. "Just tell me."

Why won't he just let me forget and move on?

With my lips pressed firmly together, I shake

my head. "Niall, trust me, you don't want to know."

His eyes widen as he grips my arm. "Not—that Brad guy—"

"No. Not him," I say hurriedly, not wanting to unintentionally dredge up those messy emotions either. But I also can't help but smile warmly at Niall's protective instinct he seems to have for me.

"Phew, dang, bro!" He breathes forcefully. "You had me panicked," he adds, putting his hand on my shoulder.

I inhale a staggered breath. Plunging into hysterics in front of Niall is the last thing I want to happen. But I feel panic rousing to life inside me, banging its way through the wall I created to keep it at bay. It will not hold much longer.

"Please tell me, so I can help," he prods softly.

Unable to maintain control, tears well in my eyes. Sniffing, I laugh my distress away. "Yeah, well, is anything in my life drama-free these days?" I gulp down hard. "I just feel stupid. Ugh, why am I crying?" I roll my eyes and wipe the tears away.

Niall squeezes my shoulder, his concern for me evident in his sorrowful eyes.

"So, um." I sniff again. "I went on a hike this morning—you know, because I like that stuff—and when I had stopped for a bit, some animals showed up."

"Animals?" he says, perplexed.

With eyes squinched, I peer at him steadfastly. *Don't make me say it*! But when his brow creases into a deep vee, I sigh. "Wolves," I whisper, even though we are the only ones around.

"Seriously?" he gasps.

Wiping my cheeks again, I nod.

"H-how are you even alive right now?" he sputters, his face a pasty white.

Heart now pounding away in my chest, I say breathlessly, "I don't know—more showed up and saved me."

"Wha-seriously?" he says, higher pitched and winded. "Unbelievable. You're-you're all right, though?" he asks in a panic, examining my body for more injuries, then cringes when he sees the long, red scratches under my arms. "Ooh dang," he winces. "That looks bad."

Though their sting lingers, I smile at him. "Looks worse than it feels."

With a face scrunched and lines of worry on his brow, Niall looks at me pressingly. "I should take you home. You don't need to be out here doing this! You should be home."

"Really. Niall, I'm fine."

He studies me a few seconds longer as if unconvinced.

"Please! I can't be home. I just want to forget it even happened!"

Slowly shaking his head, he sighs. "All right, but you better tell me when you want to leave, 'kay?"

"For sure," I agree, giving a hurried, enthusiastic nod.

"After you, then," he says, pointing the way with his outstretched arm, a small smile returning to his face, though I can still see apprehension.

"What happened there?" I say, noting the white bandage around his forearm while we make our way up the hill toward the sounds of carnival games and music.

He continues to look ahead, but a mischievous, playful smile forms out of the corner of his mouth. "Scratched it on a branch yesterday. The trees around here are vicious."

I laugh.

American and Montana State flags pattern the streets, sticking out from every light pole in town. Large signs hammered into the ground direct everyone the same way we are going. At the top of the hill, rows and rows of white and blue canopies cover the large parking lot. The food vendor trucks sit to the right of them. The smell of barbecued meat and charbroiled burgers drifts in the air with every gust of warm wind. To the left are the games—sensibly priced and plenty of them. Behind the sea of blue and white tarps is the field, crowded with model cars in all colors, shapes, and styles, from slow, antiques to fast, new ones with shiny windows that reflect the shimmering sun. The stage sits at the back of the field. The sounds of drums, trumpets, and tubas thunder from the speakers as the high school band plays their fight song. Tingles of nostalgia tickle up the back of my neck.

"So, what first?" I ask Niall as we pass a faux animal fur booth.

"We could check out stuff around here then head to the car show. Maybe grab something to eat after?"

"Excellent!" I say happily.

"Hey, Shae," he says, diverting his gaze to the ground while we walk to the first covered booth. "Umm, I just wanted to thank you again for inviting me."

"I'm the one who should be thanking you; otherwise, I'd be here alone." I smile as I pick up and examine what I believe to be a bear carved out of a piece of old driftwood. Either that or a cow; I can't quite tell which. "What even is this?"

He laughs. "Beats me."

Shrugging, I put it down and check out the keychain rock charms.

"Hey," Niall says, cocking his head to the side and smiling. "You up for a little fun? A wager, maybe?"

"What did you have in mind?" I eye him sharply, his look of mischief piquing my interest.

"Well." He picks up a hot dog-shaped squeaky toy and squeezes it. Its high-pitched, off-key horn honk makes my ears ring, and a few people look our way. "How about whoever finds the stupidest thing here," he whispers, "gets a free lunch?" Then he smiles a flirty grin. "Compliments of the loser, of course."

"Oh, you are so on!" I affirm. "Hope you brought enough money."

Determined to find the winnable oddity, we peruse for the next hour, examining every item on every table at every booth with unyielding vigor, regardless of their content. Of course, most of what we find are duds, but the distraction our little endeavor creates from the unbearable torments as of late is what truly counts.

"Ding-ding, we have a winner!" Niall calls for the umpteenth time with a smug expression of triumph as he holds up a sparkly green plastic pickle true to size.

"Eh." I shrug and sift through a pile of bandanas. "But you also said that about the last five things you showed me."

"Nuh-uh, look. See? Way stupider!" He thrusts it closer to my view. "I mean, what would someone even buy this for, anyway?"

Casually, I step away and examine the table's contents in front of me, though none of it interests me.

"Ok, well, if we are basing it on utter stupidity, then mine still trumps all yours combined!" I say, pulling out my phone. "See, that poor cat hates the unicorn horn stuck to his head even more than we do!" I add, holding up the picture for him to see.

Niall laughs hard, then looks from his item to mine and counters with a snarkier stink face.

"It's just a pickle, Niall, hardly worth the win, don't you think?"

He examines the object and sputters, "Wait! Wait, what have we here?" Then he presses a hidden button at the end. An almost incoherent song suddenly yodels out, low and slow, like a tormented duck drowning in water.

"Ewh, what is that?" I gasp.

Niall laughs energetically. "Row-row-row Your Boat, I think! See, the worst! I win!" he yells triumphantly and holds the janky object high above his head like a prized trophy.

The wobbly sound, though irritating, is also the funniest thing I've heard all day. But no way I'm telling Niall that.

"Ugh, fine, your stupid music pickle thingy wins," I relent, frowning.

"YESSS!" Niall hisses, rattling the object in my face, still pumping out the horrid sound.

Crinkling my nose at it, I shove his hand away and huff. "Stupid game anyway."

"Ah, come on, don't be like that. Your choices sucked, too," Niall says with a pouty face, then grins smugly. "But we can't all be winners."

"Gloat much, Niall?" I glare playfully. "I conceded, now drop it!" I add pointing to the table like a command to a dog playing fetch who won't give up the ball.

With a broad smile, he does as ordered. We continue down another aisle and enjoy the banter between us as we stroll with no particular destination now that our little game is done.

133

Inevitably, Niall runs into a few kids he knows from school.

The two girls in the bunch keep touching Niall's arm, laughing, and batting their long, luscious eyelashes at him. Niall starts stammering and laughing nervously. And when I think things can't get any more embarrassing for him, Niall shuffles his foot, gets it caught in a hole, and tumbles forward. Luckily, I steady him before he takes those two cutie-pie girls down. The girls cackle spiritedly, and Niall's face turns beet red.

Determined to keep him from permanently damaging his social status, I make him say goodbye and drag him away. The girls are still giggling as they wave.

Niall and I shift our direction to the field for the car show, following crowds of people with the same idea.

It has become a warm, cloudless day. The sun beats down on us, turning our exposed skin red and blotchy. Thankfully, Niall spots shade at a water station near the registration booth as we enter the makeshift bright orange gates.

"Niall, I'm curious; you like living around here?" I ask as we wait in line for water.

"It's small—way smaller than most places I've

lived."

"How many's that?" I ask as I grab a cup of water and move to the side.

"Too many to count, but I hope we stay awhile longer. I like it here." He smiles a wide, knowing grin before guzzling the water down.

"Wouldn't have anything to do with the two girls from earlier, could it?" I say with batting eyes.

His face turns bright red again.

"Pretty sure all you have to do is choose one of them," I add more genuinely.

"Uh, I don't know about that." Niall shrugs while refilling his cup from the water jug. Water splashes out fast, all over his feet.

I laugh and shake my head. "Poor kid, you have a lot to learn about girls," I warn, taking another drink. "Be careful, though. Two friends liking the same guy—means trouble!"

"I'll try and remember that." He then chugs down his second cup of water before crumpling it in his hand like a tin can.

We throw our garbage away and walk down the first row of cars. A cherry-red '57 Chevy Bel-Air Coupe with black and white dice hanging off the mirror is parked next to the local radio station's booth. The black speaker on the table blasts a hit

Beatles song so loudly that the speakers vibrate, distorting the sound. A bright canary-yellow 1967 Mustang convertible with several awards in its window glistens in the hot sun next to it.

As we meander down several rows of cars and trucks, Niall practically drools as he covetously gawks at all the sparkling, manly engines and flamed paint jobs.

Hearing my name being called from behind us, I stop and turn to see Maggie hurriedly trotting toward us. As she struts her way through the crowd, her long, curly blonde hair bounces off her shoulders. Every few steps, it falls across her square face into her large, almond-shaped blue eyes, and she flicks it away contemptuously. Her two witchy BFFs, Lauren and Abby, stride beside her as they push their way down the narrowed path.

"Ah, crap." Niall cringes. "This can't be good."

I scowl at Maggie's apparent self-importance and then take the first opportunity to blend into the crowd moving past us.

"Shae!" Maggie shrills. "Don't you walk away from me!"

"Looks like some things never change," I mumble as I stagger then stop.

Grimacing, Niall tugs at my arm like a scared

child. "Let's just get out of here," he whispers as Maggie stomps to a halt. She glares him down. Flanked by Lauren and Abby, Maggie then turns to face me.

"Maggie," I say with a placid smile.

"We need to talk." She looks at Niall and sneers, "Privately!"

"Yeah—no, here and now works better for me," I say with an eyebrow raised.

Her eyes dart over to Niall and then back to me. "Really?" she states, her voice carrying as if using a megaphone. "You sure you want to talk about what you did in front of *all* these people?" she says, pointing her long, manicured finger around.

A handful of people stop to watch us, their rumbling whispers adding to the stupidity of the situation.

"Right," I say, sardonically. "And what's that?"

Pressing her shimmering lips together, she stares at me ruthlessly for a moment, as if contemplating what to say next.

"Well, go ahead, then. What did I do?"

Uncertainty shifts in her eyes.

Knowing she's losing her nerve, I look at Niall, shrug, and we start to walk away.

"Sure thing, run away scared. Like always,"

Lauren calls nastily, like how little Yorkshire Terriers yelp and nip at your feet to make up for their lack of size. She looks thinner than usual, too.

"Excuse me?" I say, turning back around.

Abby, the lackey, steps forward. "You heard her!" she snaps, then looks at Lauren with big, brown, approval-hungry doe eyes. Lauren gives it to her in the form of a wicked grin.

"And what, exactly, am I supposed to be scared of?"

"Who do you think?" Maggie grunts, puffing up her chest, obviously finding her conviction again. Shame, I was hoping she would do the right thing for once and let the stupidity go.

"Ah . . . right," I say with a slight smile. "Well, we all know that's a load of crap."

Niall muffles a slight laugh.

"You think that's funny, Nancy?" Maggie snarls,

Hastily looking away, Niall takes a step further behind me. For a tall guy, he sure does lack the proper backbone.

"His name's Niall, and you know it," I growl.

"Whatever. Just shut up and listen," Maggie says, moving closer, our faces a few inches apart. Then, with narrow, hostile eyes, she stares me down. Well, more like up because her eye level only reaches my chin. "Stay away from my boyfriend—got it?"

The sudden laughter that spills from my lips feels so dang good that I can't help myself. "That's what this is about?" I scoff and glance at Niall, who is also trying not to smile.

"It's not funny!" Maggie screeches.

"Yeah, it kind of is because I have no idea who you're even talking about!" The statement is neither true nor false, depending on how you want to look at the facts.

"Then explain why people saw you two sneaking around behind my back!" she says, pushing my chest with her sharp, fake fingernail.

Too automatic to realize what I've done, I grab her finger and bend it back as I fling it away.

"Don't you even touch me!"

Lauren and Abby gasp in horror as Maggie's purse and contents land at the feet of the crowd.

A rumble of oohs and muffled laughter moves through the throng of oglers like a noisy wave. The whole thing suddenly feels like an immature playground brawl—nothing I would ever want to be associated with. I can feel my cheeks burning.

"Admit it, you-you homewrecker!" Maggie shrieks, holding her injured finger as though broken, while Lauren and Abby retrieve her things.

Her accusation hits so close to reality I see red. With teeth clenched so tight my jaw hurts, I step toward her. She recoils like I'm about to hit her, but I wouldn't even if I wanted to.

How dare she accuse me of such a thing? I would never!

But I know from experience arguing with her will get me nowhere.

I release the tension in my fisted hand and subdue the fiery hot rage rising inside me.

"I doubt anything I say will convince you otherwise, so feel free to believe what you want, Maggie," I whisper through my teeth, "but I haven't been sneaking around with anyone, least of all your so-called boyfriend. So, maybe the next time you get the stupid idea to accuse someone of being a cheater and not get your trash kicked in the process, you might want to go ahead and check your facts first." Then, glaring hard at Lauren and Abby, I add, "From a reliable source." To which both of them snarl back at me.

Maggie leans in again, this time not touching me. "I know you know who I'm talking about, Shae, so stop denying it. And I'm warning you, stay away from him," she hisses, so close to my face I can smell her berry lip balm.

"You sure you want to get into this right now?" I say, glancing over at Niall and then back at her. She narrows her eyes at me. "I didn't think so." I scowl. "Maybe if you're having problems with your boyfriend, you should take it up with him and leave the rest of us out of it!"

With a turn and a fist full of Niall's shirt, I drag him along as we push through the crowd.

This time, Maggie lets us leave.

Distracted by our thoughts, Niall and I move slowly twice through the food vendors' trucks lined up side by side before finally deciding on giant turkey legs and soda.

Sitting on a picnic bench facing away from the table, I lour unfocused into the crowd.

Me? Cheat with another woman's man? The idea of it makes me so livid I could punch something. I know how it feels to be lied to, to be cheated on. No way in hell would I put anyone through such pain!

Like an angry, gluttonous brute, I rip my teeth into the charred meat on a stick clutched in my hand; the juices drip on the ground at my feet.

Worst of all, a cheating scandal is precisely what I've been trying to avoid. And Maggie makes me the villain in her messed-up, fake relationship! Thanks a lot, Maggie!

"Niall, stop it," I mumble through a mouthful of food after watching him take his third quick glance in my direction. "What, do I have food on my face or something?" To be sure, I pat the napkin around my mouth.

"Can't I look at you without having a reason?"

"Not unless you're looking to be smacked," I snigger.

He picks at his meat stick and then another peek at me.

"*Niall!*" I huff. "What?"

Puffing air heavily from the corner of his frowning mouth, he sighs, "You're not letting what she said get to you, are you?"

"What? Her empty threats? Not likely," I say, tearing another piece of meat off the bone with my front teeth.

"No, about Marcas cheating on her with you."

The bluntness of his statement sends a jolt of anger like a lightning bolt charging through me.

"I swear, they're not dating. And I know for a fact he'd never cheat on anyone. He's not like—"

"Niall, it's none of my business what he does or doesn't do."

"Yeah, but it makes me so mad that she says he's capable of it."

"If you know he wouldn't, what does it matter what she says?"

"Because it makes him look bad, and others might believe her!"

The truth of it hits hard. The very fear he speaks of, I know it well. But at the same time, what did he expect? His brother dated Maggie, for crap's sake! Pulling this stuff is all she does. But telling Niall as much would hardly help, so I say nothing.

We sit in silence for a few minutes until I see him have a look-see at me again.

"Niall! Seriously. What?" I say, staring at him sternly.

"You're different from most girls," he says quietly, almost awestruck.

I laugh. "Why, because I eat what I want when I want and how I want and can still look this fabulous?" I say with a sarcastic smirk.

"Hardly!" he chuckles, but then his face turns solemn. "Because of how fearless you are. You've been through so much lately, and it doesn't seem to even affect you. It's pretty cool, actually. I mean the being strong about it, not the having it happen part." Then, holding his turkey leg like a caveman, he rips a piece off with his teeth and chews it contemplatively.

Uncomfortable with his unmerited praises, I swallow my bite with a heavy gulp. "Don't make me out to be more than I am, Niall," I say more seriously than I've ever been with him. "I was terrified—every time!"

He shakes his head. "Ok, yeah, but still, half the stuff you've dealt with would make most people, even some men, cry like babies and run away screaming. Not you, though; you're still standing. Still came out with me."

"Who says I didn't cry?" My words dangle there for him to grasp their magnitude. I watch his eyes shift, a hint of regret in them; from bringing it up or something different altogether, I don't know. "If anything, my willingness to forgo any sort of reluctance shows I lack the brains to make smart choices," I mumble cynically as I wipe my chin and look out at the crowd. "Believe me, I'm still totally freaked . . . about all of it."

He sighs heavily. "You know, Shae, bravery doesn't mean you don't get scared." He smiles warmly at me. "And you don't fool me. I saw how you handled Maggie today. Talk about scary."

"She was, wasn't she?" I let a smile form on my

face.

"I thought she'd claw your eyes out, pull your hair, or whatever happens when girls fight."

I laugh aloud, imagining myself lunging onto Maggie's back and ripping out her long, curly locks by the fistfuls like some wild animal.

Seeing my sudden change in mood, Niall joins in with a robust laugh as if he is picturing it too.

"What are you laughing at? You were no help." I glare in playful disappointment at him.

He laughs hard—too hard—then inhales sharply. "Yeah, not a chance."

Getting up, I toss my trash in the garbage and wipe as much grease off my hands as possible. I give up when the grease acts like glue, adhering to the cheap napkins and leaving small pieces behind.

"Ready?"

He nods in agreement.

While we shimmy past the ticket booths and over to the game area, a large crowd forms around the ring toss. Its line wraps around the corner of another game, ending in front of the beanbag toss. Players hit their target, and then walk away with a stuffed animal, a plastic blowup sword, or a lightsaber.

Neither of us is in the mood to play, but we

continue wandering for a while anyway. Watching everyone else enjoy themselves has a calming effect on both of us.

We had just walked past the dunk tank when Sam and Finn came running.

"Dude, answer your damn phone!" Sam growls, heaving in deep breaths. Glancing at me, he adds a "Hey, Shae," with a nod, then looks back at Niall. "We've been looking all over for you, man. Marcas is pissed!"

Grimacing, Niall mumbles what can only be an array of choice words he wishes to keep to himself as he takes out his phone. "I forgot to turn the ringer back on."

"You idiot," Sam says, glaring. "Didn't he specifically tell you to make sure?"

Consumed by texts, Niall ignores Sam.

"Is everything okay?" I ask after watching Finn and Sam exchange a look of annoyance that had quickly shifted to concern.

Finn smiles the tenseness away. "Yeah, just something happened earlier that Marcas is still bent out of shape about it. Nothing to worry about."

Sam quickly punches him in the arm and harshly whispers too quietly to overhear.

"Oh. Do you think you'll still make it tonight,

then?" I ask, and they both look at me.

"Uh, yeah, I hope so," Finn says, scrunching his forehead and smiling, "but I'll let Jamie know if things change." And with that, he's back to conversing with Sam.

Something about the hesitation I see in his eyes tells me he should have just told me no. And the way they try to downplay their supposed non-issue only magnifies my curiosity.

A nagging knot of worry forms in my stomach as I watch Finn and Sam take suspiciously quick checks at the surrounding crowd, like danger lurks in those walking by.

I look at Niall. His eyes narrow on the phone's screen, and he huffs angrily.

"Hey, Niall."

He doesn't reply.

"Niall, listen, if you have to go—"

"Right!" he grumbles, snarling. "Not gonna happen." Then he shoves his phone into his back pocket and gives me a wink.

"Hey, listen, I got an idea," he says to his brothers smugly. "How about you two go run off and let Marcas know that I'm, you know, kind of busy here?" He shoots a sly smirk at me, then looks back at his brother. "I mean, you all are more than capable of handling stuff, right? And if not, then you can all come find me again later!" His tone, though light and playful, runs thick with sour intent. "Sound good?" He grins at them mockingly.

"Sure," Finn scoffs. "You got some kind of death wish? 'Cause I sure as hell don't!"

"Will you just come on? Don't make us drag you away." Sam glares.

"Go *away*," Niall says sharply. "You don't even need me anyway." Then he reaches over, turns my body around by the shoulders, and rests his arm there as we walk away.

"That probably wasn't a good idea," I say as we head for the safety of the crowd.

"Meh," he scoffs with a smile and keeps walking.

We round the corner of the dart booth like we are running from the law and abruptly stop—Marcas stands in wait as though expecting us is Marcas.

Breathing heavily and hair askew, Marcas stares hard at Niall, his eyes smoldering with anger.

The unsettling tension between them grows thick like a sudden storm shifting in the air. I pull my shoulder sluggishly away from Niall and step back. His arm falls limp to his side.

"Where do you think you're going, Niall?" Marcas says darkly.

"Shae and I were just going to get ice cream," Niall lies. "Di-did you want to join us?"

The subtle mention of my name makes me want to find the nearest rock and climb under it. It's awkward enough witnessing this go down, but to be used as the excuse? Ugh.

"This isn't a game, Niall, and you know it. This behavior, this juvenile disregard, isn't like you." Marcas' eyes shift for a second in my direction.

My body tenses. Hold on. I'm to blame for this?

"But—"

"No!" Marcas booms, his deep, aggressive tone making Niall physically jolt.

Chills take over my entire body.

I don't know if it's seeing Niall's shoulders crumple into a pitiful slouch or the fact that I am fed up with Marcas and his arrogant, dominating power he seems to yield like he has all the right to, but I cannot hold my tongue any longer.

When Niall starts to move away from me, I tug him back by the arm.

"Now, hold on a sec," I say sharply. "Seriously, Marcas, look around. There's literally a celebration happening here. Can't Niall hang out a little longer?"

Marcas finally considers me. His hard, loathsome-filled eyes tell me to back off, yet they still somehow cause my insides to turn to mush.

"No, he can't." He scowls.

"Why not? Can't he be a kid for one measly second without you barking at him like some overbearing buzzkill?"

His eyes narrow. "You sure have a lot to say about something you have no business being a part of."

"Get over yourself." I glare. "Not everything is life or death, Marcas! He's just a kid wanting to have a little fun."

As soon as I realize what I have said, remembering their father, I regret it.

"Look, little girl," he jabs, "you don't know anything about us, and you damn well don't know what's best for Niall, so stop sticking your nose where it doesn't belong!"

Niall cringes.

Outwardly, I glare so hard my eyes lose focus, but on the inside, the bluntness of his words and the undercutting of my age and gender smack me right in the heart. What a jerk!

Forced by Marcas' hard stare, I gulp down the

rumbling storm of fury shifting inside me. I watch him closely, looking for any sign of good in him, and wonder if I will ever actually see any.

Looking from me to Niall, Marcas then yells over the game booth directly behind us, "Sam, Finn, let's go!"

Niall drops his head and will not look at me again. When Sam and Finn come running, they all leave without another word.

Ferocity courses through my blood like a river of hot, bubbling lava in my veins. How dare Marcas treat Niall like that, or me, for that matter? Who does he think he is?

With their secrets and suspicious behavior, it's obvious they are hiding something. No one gets that upset about missed text messages.

Jamie! The idea pops into my head like popcorn. She has to know what all this is about. But then my excitement plummets, realizing she won't be off until later.

Time—left with the bothersome predicament of having too much of it, I debate what to do.

I settle on doing nothing, and I'm positive I won't survive the wait.

CHAPTER 8

THE UNEXPECTED

The back door to the flower shop softly squeaks as I open it and step inside. Muffled voices subtly waft through the thin crack in the curtains separating the prep room from the showroom out front. Closing the door slowly, I walk to the room's threshold. Peeking through the space in the thick fabric, I see Jamie talking with a tall, slender man with broad, thick shoulders. Stiffly postured, he stands with his back to me, arms folded.

"That's not what I asked you!" he says, unfolding his burly arms and moving closer to Jamie. "And it would be *very* foolish to keep wasting my time. Especially since I made it quite clear what could happen if you did."

"You don't have to get all testy about it!" Jamie huffs as she hurries around to the back side of the counter. "And would it kill you to say please for once? It's called manners!"

When he approaches the counter's edge, Jamie takes a step back.

"Look, I've already told you I haven't seen her, and I don't plan to."

"I presume you to be an intelligent girl, so don't go acting the fool now." He then looks out the window at the two men standing outside facing the street. "I would hate for it to get crowded in here."

"All right—fine," she grunts. "The last time I saw her, she said she'd be out of town for a few days—camping, fishing, or something like that. We're not exactly friends, so I didn't bother for details."

Friend? What friend?

"Interesting," he says calmly—I assume, more to himself because he is still looking out the window. "And you think I will believe such a load of garbage, do you?" Turning to the side, I finally see a portion of his face. His narrowed eye has no warmth. A chill runs through me. Who is he?

"Why not? It's the truth," she barks back, but the sudden, higher-pitched tone to her voice gives way to her nerves.

For a moment, he ponders her.

"Such loyalty you have, to risk discomfort for her. I hope she values your friendship as much as you do hers." Then he looks to the window again. "I suppose it doesn't matter. Eventually, she will readily seek me out." Then he leaves the store, his words of affirmation echoing in my ears.

Not realizing I had been clutching the curtains in my hands, I let go and shift half a step back from the opening; rushing through, Jamie slams into me.

We both let out high-pitched shrieking screams in unison.

"What are you doing here?" she gasps, clutching the door frame and her chest. "You nearly gave me a heart attack."

"Sorry," I pant. "I thought I'd come a little early."

"Wait, have you been here the whole time?" she asks, a flash of alarm in her eyes.

"Only just," I say, leaning against the workbench for support.

"Oh," she says, standing up straight and smiling. "You ready to go, then?" She swirls me around, gingerly moving us further into the back room.

"Wait, Jamie, who was that?"

"I don't know, some old dude," she shrugs.

"He was looking for someone? Someone you know?" I say, gulping down worry as she drags me along.

She looks at me concerned. "You could say that." Then she smiles a little. "But don't worry, I told him nothin'. No business of his where you are."

"Wha-me?" I ask while I struggle to shove the panic I feel trying to surface inside me.

She grabs my arm and pulls me to the back door. "Yeah, you piss someone off lately or somethin'?"

A cold chill moves down my spine as I think of only one willing to track me down.

"You said older? Not like our age or anything?"

"Huh, not even close. Sound like someone you know?" She stops walking, mumbles something about needing to lock the front door, then turns around and leaves me in the doorway, nibbling my nail while she does it.

Could Brad have sent someone to find me?

"No one comes to mind," I affirm after a moment as she locks the door and then double-checks to confirm it is secure.

"I wouldn't worry about it, Shae," she says as she weaves through the display tables and then grabs her phone and purse off the prep table before stopping in front of me, a smirkish grimace on her face. "Besides, if it was that important, he could have been much nicer about it. He's probably just got the old geezer constipation grumps. Eat some prunes, why don't ya?" She laughs as she goes to the back door.

I hesitantly follow.

Peeking out the curtain covering the back window, I add, "Hope you're right," and wonder if she would be so dismissive if she knew what had happened to me recently.

We step onto the loading dock, and Jamie locks the deadbolt on the door behind us.

"Is that a cast on your arm or a failed fashion accessory?" she asks coolly as we reach the bottom stairs to the left and start down the alley.

I chuckle, not surprised by her lack of concern. Scrapes, bruises, and the occasional sprained something or other after a hike are often expected from me.

"Want the long version or the short?" She looks at me impatiently, and I laugh. "It's not broken. I'm fine." I smile. "Hey, have you heard from Finn lately?"

"Doh, yes. I forgot to read his text," she says, pulling out her phone. "Says we're supposed to meet in front of the games in a few minutes. Aw, adorbs, he wants to win me a big stuffed animal!" she adds, hugging the phone to her chest. "What a sweetie pie!" Then she quickly sends a reply. When the main screen appears, a close-up picture of them hugging shows front and center.

"Ooh, look at you two love birds!" I say, swiping the phone from her hand. She tries jumping in the air to grab it from my outstretched arm as I examine their cuteness, but she is too short to get it away from me.

"You guys really are the cutest," I add, giving a pleasing smile as I hand back the phone.

"He's amazing, isn't he?" she beams, letting out a big dreamy sigh.

"Speaking of meeting up, did I tell you I met their brother, Niall?" I say as we turn down another road and head up a big hill.

"He's scrawny, isn't he?" Then, looking at me, she grins. "And kind of awkward?"

"Not really. I think he's kind of sweet. We sort of hung out today."

"That's cool, I guess. Better than staying home alone."

"Yeah, we walked around mostly, but it was still fun. I kind of invited him tonight; figured you'd be fine with it."

She looks at me hard, scrutiny in her eyes.

"It's not like that, Jamie. We're just friends, and he knows it."

"Hope so, you cradle robber," she says, elbowing my arm. But before I can react, someone calls her from behind.

"Jamie!" Finn yells again and wraps his arms around her waist, spinning her in a circle.

Though disheartened, my moment of opportunity for intel passing, I smile anyway. They are too cute not to be a little happy for them.

Standing beside them, Niall diverts his gaze, avoiding eye contact with everyone, even me.

Moving beside him, I nudge his shoulder with mine. "Hey!"

He gives a deflated, limp wave and smiles, but it fades too quickly to be genuine.

"How much trouble are you in?" I ask, resting my good hand on his shoulder.

It takes a minute for him to even look at me.

"The usual amount, I guess," he grumbles like a

scolded child.

The sadness in his eyes makes my heart hurt. "You sure about that?" He shrugs, and I let my hand fall from his shoulder. "Want to talk about it?"

He shrugs lazily again and exhales heavily. "I'm just sorry about Marcas."

The mention of his name sends me sudden flutters of warm feelings, and I cringe. They have no business being there, especially with how livid I am with him.

"I don't want you to hate him. He's a good guy, I promise," Niall says quietly. "Just dealing with a lot right now."

"Niall, I don't hate him. But what he said—how he said it—is not okay."

Niall's frown deepens, as if it could even get any poutier.

"Come on, Niall, I'm fine!" I poke him in the ribs to get him to smile, but it doesn't work. "Really, all good here."

"Wait, I'm confused—who is this again?" Finn asks Jamie, his voice carrying enough that Niall and I cannot help but overhear.

Niall looks at me, confused.

"Finn, really." She puts her hand on his arm. "It was just some guy."

He looks at her firmly, as if she said something ironic.

"What?" She shrugs.

A little smile forms on his lips. "Well, did he have a name? Was he there for a reason or just to harass my girlfriend?"

She snickers for what I believe is the use of the word *girlfriend* again and shakes her head. "Just looking for Shae."

When Finn looks at me, his large eyes, full of unease, soften when he sees me listening.

A shiver runs through me. Does Finn know about Brad? And believe it has something to do with him, too?

Finn pulls Jamie closer. "I hate that he was unkind to you." She rests her head on his shoulder as he wraps his arms around her. "Call next time, and I'll come take care of it, 'kay?"

Her smile grows three sizes when he kisses her cheek, then abruptly sags after he whispers in her ear. Taking a step back from her, he pulls out his phone, quickly sends a text, then shoots Niall a stern look before hurrying toward the back of the parking lot.

"Hey, Jamie, everything good?" I say as she bites her fingernail, still watching him go.

"Sure." She looks at me briefly with a pressed smile. "He'll be right back." Then she turns to watch kids talking by the cotton candy booth.

"Jamie," I say, on edge, knowing sudden silence isn't like her.

She doesn't answer.

"Jamie?"

"Mm-hm," she replies robotically, almost as if she can't snap out of a trance. Then, mumbling something about getting a better view, she walks closer to the darts game a few feet away.

"'Kay? Guess I'll just stand here by myself, then?" I grumble aloud, though no one around seems to care. I look at Niall, standing alone and shifting his feet nervously back and forth as he stares blankly into the crowd, and I walk over.

"Did you just see that? Zombie Jamie over there?" I snort in a whisper.

All I get is a slight shake of the head, so minuscule, it very well could have been a tick or involuntary twitch and nothing more.

What is with everyone right now?

"You don't think all this is about Brad, do you, Niall?" I whisper, leaning in closer.

His head pops up, eyes wild. Then, as they go lax, the melancholy returning, he shakes his head and mumbles, "No," quietly.

The single, monotone answer irritates me.

With nothing more said, we wait. I don't know for what, but I find myself wishing the awkward night would just end and put me out of my misery.

When Finn eventually returns, he whispers something to Jamie, and she smiles and giggles. Then when his phone chimes, he lets her read the message.

Squealing with excitement, she comes running over to me, a smile wider than the Grand Canyon strung across her face.

"What's with you?" I tease with appalled mockery while eyeing her closely.

"What do you mean?" she asks innocently.

"You're serious, right? You've been a complete bum! Wandering off, saying nothing to me for like ten minutes now, and suddenly you're all happy again?"

"I did not!"

"Uh, yeah, you did!" I laugh. "Like some love-sick girl without her man. Meanwhile, I'm here, doing nothing—"

"I know; I'm sorry. Finn sort of had me worried for a minute. Marcas wanted them to go back to work or something."

"And now?"

She tries to smother her evil, mischievous smile by pressing her lips together, but I still see it in her eyes.

"What?"

She laughs. "It's just that Sam and Marcas have decided to come with us, too! That will be fun, right?"

"Right. Sure it will," I add sardonically, knowing it will be anything but. "Wait, why are you so happy about this? Aren't they crashing your *date*?"

"What, no! The more, the merrier!" Interweaving our arms, she shakes us excitedly. "This is going to be great!" Then she squeezes my arm.

I nod, trying to mirror her enthusiasm with a smile, but I fail miserably because I am anything but excited. Too happy to notice, she pulls us closer to Finn and Niall.

Thinking about spending the rest of the evening around Marcas makes my stomach twist and turn like I've eaten a dozen bean burritos. Which one of him will I encounter this time? The cryptic, disgruntled one? The sweet, concerned brother of a friend? Maybe, if I'm lucky, he'll even avoid me altogether. It would definitely make for a more bearable time.

But then again, what if he attempts a decent conversation with me for once? Worse things could happen, I guess. And then I shudder as Marcas' angry words echo in my mind. On second thought, distance is way better—and as long as he doesn't show me those gorgeous green eyes of his, I just might be able to follow through with it.

Finn pulls the trigger on the rifle, sending the tiny BB at his target. A loud ding rings out as it hits the mark. Then, with rapid fire, he hits everything he shoots at.

Jamie bounces up and down in excitement when the booth attendant retrieves Finn's prize from the top of a mesh wall covered with stuffed animals and hands it to him. Finn smiles and gives Jamie the stuffed monkey wearing a red and white polka-dotted bow tie, holding a banana up to its ear like a phone. She hugs it to her chest and grins. As they walk to the next game holding hands, a twinge of jealousy tugs at me. I love that she has found someone, but in doing so, I have now become the metaphorical third wheel.

"You're being extra quiet," Niall whispers, walking in stride next to me. "You still worried it's Brad?"

"What—so, you're talking now?" I ask, stopping in front of the basketball toss.

"Maybe. You going to stop gnawing your lower lip long enough to answer?"

"I wasn't—" I say, pressing my lips together and then licking them, "thinking about him."

"Then what's the matter?" He leans in closer to my face and smiles. "I know there's something."

Finding his persistence humorous, I smirk and playfully shove him back. "Just stuff."

"Like what? Marcas?"

"What? No!" I say a little too sharply. "Why would you even think that?" I can feel my face turning red.

"Umm, because of earlier," he says, raising an eyebrow.

"Oh, right," I mumble, feeling incredibly stupid for overreacting. "Actually, I was just wondering what else could go wrong today? Take the popcorn stand over there, for example. Could burst into flames right when we pass by, or not. Who knows? But with my luck, most likely."

He laughs.

I join in, and for a moment, I forget what's bothering me—which is, in fact, Marcas.

"Mmm, popcorn! You want some?" Niall asks,

pointing with his head to the popcorn trolley. I frown, and he smiles coyly. "Don't worry, I got you. You stay here, where it's safe." He tries patting my head like a puppy.

"Watch yourself," I taunt, dodging his hand.

He backs away slowly, grinning, then turns before becoming lost in the crowd.

While I wait, I watch a couple of guys try their luck at the basketball toss. They step up to the line wearing hats backward and their purple rip-off pants sagging so low they could double as thigh-high socks.

Balls to their chest, they toss them as forcefully as their scrawny arms can muster. But the oversized ball bounces off the oblong rim and back at them, hitting one square in the head while the other trips over his pants to get at the ball as it bounces away.

As I silently snicker at their play, someone walks up beside me, clearing their throat as they do.

Gripping his hands on the chain-link fence, Marcas lets out a soft chuckle that makes my body stiffen. Then, out of the corner of my eye, I see him glance at me before watching the wannabe ball players shoot the ball.

Marcas shakes his head. "What are they even doing?"

"Trying to be cool," I reply automatically, then cringe for forgetting my pact not to talk to him.

"They aren't doing a very good job, now, are they?" he adds, stifling a laugh as he looks down at me, his eyes twinkling and his smile wide. It makes my insides flip-flop.

Looking back at the boys, I say coolly, "Nope. And they look ridiculous." Then I sputter-laugh when one of them loses their pants when jumping to make a shot.

Unable to help myself, I look at Marcas when I hear him laughing too. His warm, genuine smile remains a moment longer before fading as he stares more knowingly at me. Again, I look away—not interested in the game but afraid of what I see in the depths of his eyes.

Knowing he is watching me, my heart beats wildly in my chest.

"Shae, can I talk to you for a second?" he finally says softly, his tone sad.

"Uh, sure," I say unsurely, having no idea what I am getting myself into.

Gingerly touching my elbow, he guides me a few feet further from Jamie, Finn, and Sam, who are distracted by the ping-pong ball toss. When we stop at a bench by the goldfish display, he turns to face me, though his eyes do not meet mine. He is nervous, and I like that he is; it means whatever he is about to say will not be easy. And after the way he has been toward me, I welcome the change I see.

"I want to apologize for my behavior earlier," he says quietly.

The plinking of plastic rings on glass bowls in the distance creates a musical melody that threatens to lure me away in thought. But I doubt even an earthquake at this moment could take my attention away from the man before me.

"I should not have raised my voice to you like that. No matter what I was dealing with or the reason, you didn't deserve such behavior, and I am so very sorry."

His eyes, beaming at me, sparkle with a hint of reluctance. I gulp down the unease I feel. His remorse seems so unlike him, so startlingly genuine, that I don't know how to react. Then his sharp, angry "little girl" words ring in my head, stinging as painfully as the first time he said them.

Nodding, I look slightly away from him.

Can I trust Marcas? Trust the realness I see in him, or will he snap back to the one whose behavior cuts deep?

"I had no business butting in," I say quietly, "I

should have never—"

"No, you were only looking out for Niall. I realize that now." He gives a slight smile from the corner of his mouth. "Unfortunately, I tend to be a little touchy when it comes to my family. Prefer to keep things private. Not one of my better qualities, I'm afraid. And it gets the best of me sometimes," he says genuinely. "But it's nice that you care for Niall, though. He's lucky to have found such a friend! He seems to be in short supply these days."

I frown. "But he's so easy to talk to, to hang out with!"

He shrugs. "All things I have told him repeatedly, and yet he still thinks he's somehow intimidating."

I suppress a laugh. Dorky, playful, humorous, yes, but intimidating? Then I think back to the group of kids from earlier and realize that the boys hadn't said a word to Niall while the girls hung all over him. Oddly enough, I hadn't noticed it before. It makes me sad for him.

"I know it might not mean much, but I am truly sorry," Marcas says, taking a step to make us closer.

"No, I know," I say, guarded.

"And I'm afraid if you don't forgive me, Niall might hold it against me for the rest of my life!"

I smile, knowing just how much that sounds like him. But then my face turns serious again. Slowly, I step away from Marcas and grip the back of the bench in front of me for support.

"Please, Shae." He places his hand on top of mine, and a spark of warmth shoots through my body. It startles me, and I know he notices it.

Swallowing down my nerves, I feel my throat already constricting.

"Marcas?" Calling him by name makes my insides turn somersaults, "I, uh, I was kind of wondering if you could explain something to me." I gently pull my hand out from under his, knowing I would not be able to focus if it remained.

Ignoring my sudden withdrawal, he shifted his weight from one leg to the other. "Of course, anything."

"The other night when Jamie introduced us, why—" I gulp hard, my mouth so dry I could choke on my tongue.

Marcas' eyes narrow with concern at me.

"Why did you not—I just figured since what happened between us. I mean, I don't mean anything happened between us." My chest constricts, my heart pounding so rapidly I may pass out. "I just—"

"Shae," Marcas grabs my hand again and squeezes it. His touch is so charged with pounding magnetism that I hear my heart beating in my ears. "You were upset, and rightly so, but Jamie didn't know that. And it was neither the time nor the place to speak of it. So, I stayed back, so as not to upset you further or give the indication that something had happened between us."

"Oh!" I say, surprised, my cheeks growing warm. Niall *was* right!

"Yeah, tha-that makes sense. I mean, I guess I just wanted to talk to you about it, but you left so fast I couldn't. And then upstairs—" I shrug my shoulders and look down. "I just thought maybe I had done something. That what had happened—"

Marcas tilts my chin up so I can look him in the eyes. "You did nothing wrong." He presses his lips together in thought. "I'm sorry. I didn't realize my actions would come off as indifference. I only wanted to protect you. To save you from more pain."

Marcas wanted to protect me?

He looks deeper into my eyes, making me fall further into his gaze.

A tear drips down my face.

"No, don't—don't do that," he says, pulling me

into his arms. Strong, warm, and comforting, they wrap around me tightly.

I just stand there, unmoving and unsure of what to do. Soon, I give in to it, my arms finding their way around his firm upper body.

"Truly, I never meant to upset you more," he whispers.

"I know," I whisper back, unable to say anything more with his strong hands around my back and the warmth of his chest against me.

Caught up in Marcas' touch, time loses its hold on me.

A fake cough from behind me brings us quickly back to the present.

Flushed with warmth, I swiftly move from Marcas and see Niall standing a foot away, holding a bag of popcorn in one hand and a 32-ounce soda in the other. While watching me, a crooked smile widens on his smug face.

I know what he is thinking, but I am not interested in Marcas—or at least that is what I try to convince myself of when I rush by Niall toward the field.

"What are you gawking at?" I gripe hurriedly.

I swear I hear him laugh, but I'm too embarrassed to look back.

"We've already set up blankets for the show. You don't have to run away so fast," Niall yells with a mocking, *'I'll never let you live this down'* sort of tone.

When I catch up with Jamie, she simply smiles at me, which leads me to believe she's been too infatuated with Finn in their little bliss bubble to have noticed what had just happened.

The setting sun creates a yellow, orange, and red tint to the surrounding field, its artistic hues bouncing off the mountains beyond us. All around the grassy field, people sit on chairs and blankets and, in one area, on metal bleachers.

A large group of teenagers with faces painted red, white, and blue play a game of two-hand-touch football in an open area of the field. Kids wearing glow-in-the-dark rings around their necks and arms weave in and around the blankets at the center of the field, playing tag. From somewhere distant, the slight smell of campfires blows in the air.

As I step lightly through the sea of people like a ballerina on point, I replay my moment with Marcas in my head. His kind words and the soft feel of his touch linger as if they are happening all over again. Dreamily, I wander toward Sam on a spot just right of center field. On his back, hands behind his head, he lies on the blanket, staring into the evening sky.

"Yo, Shae, how's it goin'?" he asks, glancing over at me, "Where're the others? They coming or what?" His eyes casually look past me for them. That's when I notice a small scratch just under his left eye. It's minuscule enough but seems to stick out against his blue eyes. It looks faded and old, but I do not remember it being there earlier.

"Finn and Jamie stopped for snacks, and the other two are right behind me," I say, using my splinted hand to point.

"Ooh, man, your arm!" He winces, flicking his blonde hair out of his face while shifting to see me better. "I heard what happened. Bet it hurts."

"A little." I smile, though it surprises me that he knows. How much had Niall actually told him?

Sam then comments about the clear sky, the warm temperatures, and something else about summer nights being a great time to find chics. But then the conversation quickly fizzles, so I sit down just as the others walk up. Jamie and Finn lounge on the blanket by Sam, while Niall comes around and sits to my right, sharing the blanket with me. He moves in close, his crooked smile in my face. I roll my eyes and playfully shove his shoulder.

Popcorn scatters across the blanket and into the grass.

"Hey, no wasting good popcorn!" he exclaims, bending like a contortionist for the pieces.

Far behind us, the lead singer of a band strums his guitar strings, testing the sound system with a "one, two, one, two." Suddenly, their familiar beat blares through the speakers around the field.

"Yeah! All right! It's my jam!" Sam yells with excitement to Finn, who seems too busy tangling his fingers with Jamie's to give more than a quick, sarcastic expression, making Sam snarl.

It looks like I'm not the only one who dislikes being left out.

Marcas sits down on the far side of Jamie and Finn, and though he sees where I am, he smiles and then turns his attention to the band.

My heart rises and then falls in my chest like a roller-coaster ride.

Did I misread him? Was it out of sympathy alone that he comforted me? Did he not feel what I felt when he held me?

Ugh, why? Why, for the love of all that is good, do girls fantasize about an interaction with a boy, dissecting every moment to the point of losing all reality?

Needing to stop the madness in my brain, I gaze out at the swarming crowd. Limited areas of the field are still visible. The chill in the air dips faster the more the sun sets.

"Psst, Shae?" Jamie whispers and smiles wide as she tilts her head at the couple several feet in front of us, going at it like rabbits, rubbing their hands all over each other.

I stretch my lips wide in a silent cringe.

She rolls her eyes and mouths, "Get a room." Her nose scrunching as she hands me a piece of red licorice. Eating it slowly, I watch the crowd continue to gather.

Turning to grab another piece of candy, I find Marcas, having moved next to me while I was distracted.

I smile at the happy look on his face.

"This should be fun, right?" He settles in closer, our bodies inches from each other, his heat warming me.

Behind him, I catch a glimpse of Jamie, her thumb dorkily pointing up excitedly. I squirm in my seat and ignore her.

"Yeah, should be. My dad said they were able to get some huge fireworks this year."

"I heard that." He peers into the night sky then

down at me because even when sitting, he's still much taller than me. "Ever been to New York? Now, there's a fireworks show."

"Nope, never. But my cousin has. Three years in a row. Maybe someday I will, though."

With his green eyes gleaming in the setting sun, he shrugs. "Nah, too crowded. Here's perfect. Plenty of space to sit and enjoy the show." He nudges my arm, leaving a tingly feeling behind.

"Exactly," I say, feeling as if there is nowhere else I'd rather be at this exact moment.

He grins. "Niall said you—"

"Don't look now, Marcas," Sam says, abruptly sitting up, an impish grin on his lips. "Crazy stalker heading this way, and man, does she look pissed."

Marcas's body tenses, his smile suddenly gone.

Finn laughs. "Ooh, you're in for it now, dude!"

"This should entertain," Sam adds, rubbing his hands together zealously, a huge smile plastered on his face.

The gentle evening breeze chills me, and I shudder as I shoot Niall a nervous glance. With his lips in a firm, straight line, he shrugs his shoulders and scrunches his brow with apprehension.

Suddenly, I realize where I'm sitting. Too late to make a run for it; I have no choice but to brace for

177

another ugly Maggie encounter.

"Hey, guys! Fun night, huh?" Maggie asks in a surprisingly sweet voice.

No one reacts, and everyone but Marcas sits there staring at her.

She makes a nervous little laugh and clears her throat. "Hey, uh, Marcas, can I talk to you over here for a sec?" She points behind her with her thumb.

Marcas finally looks up at her but makes no effort to move.

Maggie's smile sags. "Please," she begs in a high-pitched voice that aggravates like the blaring sirens of an emergency vehicle. While twirling her glossy hair around her index finger, she looks at him longingly. "Just for a minute?"

"Maggie, we've been over this," Marcas says, his voice firm yet polite.

"Just one minute, I promise. Then you can go back to—" she trails off while eyeing everyone with slight disgust.

"I don't think that's a good idea."

"But I know that if we just talk, we can work this out!"

"There's nothing more to say, and you know it."

"I can change. I promise. Give me a chance to show you I can!" Her eyes shift slightly, looking out of the corner of her eye at me.

Having tried hard not to laugh, Sam and Finn suddenly let out sputtering laughter. Jamie jabs Finn in the stomach with her elbow, making him cough and laugh at once.

Marcas glares at them, and they hurriedly cover their mouths to silence themselves. When Marcas looks back at Maggie, his eyes hold a hint of remorse behind them.

"It won't change anything, Maggie. I think it's best if you just go."

I almost feel sorry for her, being vulnerable and exposing herself so openly. But my sympathy vanishes when I remember how miserable she has made me countless times.

As if to prove my point, all the niceness suddenly drains from her face. Like a mask being ripped away, exposing the monster beneath, hatred flashes in her eyes as they narrow in on me. Then her eyes dart back to Marcas.

"You'll regret this, Marcas! And don't think I'll come running the second you realize what a horrendous mistake you've made."

He blinks blankly back at her.

She opens her mouth to say something else but growls in frustration instead. While flipping her hair aggressively, she turns on her pink high heels, huffs loudly, and stomps off.

I hide my smile under the corner of my blanket, not wanting anyone to see. But after such a public display, there is no denying Maggie and Marcas are over, and everyone knows it—especially me.

CHAPTER 9

IN A NEW LIGHT

Tax, attached to the leash in my hand, tugs me along as I inattentively walk down the street.

Last night's events have taken over my every waking thought. How it felt to have Marcas and his warmth so close to me; the flutters of excitement that palpitated in my chest whenever he looked at me with happy green eyes—all linger in me as if having happened only moments ago.

I had wanted to go back to our conversation, before Maggie interrupted, but we never got the chance. Soon after, the band started playing, and the fireworks went off, leaving Marcas' half-asked question unfinished and dampening any hope of furthering our connection.

Marcas remained by my side, sharing a blanket while pointing out his favorite fireworks. But for me, they were nothing but an afterthought. His eyes, smile, and how our bodies slowly inched closer to each other, though they never seemed to touch, had been all the excitement I needed. And yet when we finally did touch, it was like our own personal fireworks show.

It surprised me how much I liked being there with him and how my feelings for him seemed to grow as the night went on.

At one point, all I could think about was his hand, inches from mine, screaming for me to reach over and take it. I was so nervous my chest ached, but I couldn't get myself to try. Not if there was a chance he would reject it.

The evening seemed to fly by, and before I knew it, Marcas and Niall were walking me home. Niall did most of the talking. I humored him, keeping the conversation going as best I could, but my heart wasn't in it. Marcas was silent again, even more distracted than usual, and I didn't know why. I wanted him to say something—anything—but his silence persisted, causing me a great deal of displeasure.

Ultimately, I had to settle for a goodnight smile

and the typical *'see you later'* reply. Far from the goodbye I had hoped for. Honestly, I don't know what I expected with Niall there, but anything would have been better than what I was left with. The tormenting idea of an "us" that could be forming—what is and what might be, the anticipation, the expectations, the potential opportunities before us—has me in a frenzy and greedy for answers. And are also the very reason I am letting Tax drag me through town without bothering where we might end up.

Tax slows to a stop in front of metal double doors. A familiar-looking decal of a giant abstract-shaped eagle with a blue background separated by the door's divide comes into focus.

I smile. "Good boy, Tax!" I say, ruffling his head. It's reassuring to know if I were to ever lose my mind, Tax has one sharp enough for the both of us.

Inside the building, I make my way to the mailbox, insert the key, and retrieve its contents.

"You think it'll rain?" Marcas asks, making me drop my magazine. "Ooh, sorry about that." He smiles and bends down to retrieve it. When he hands it to me, our hands touch.

"Boy, you Brannons sure like to catch a girl off guard, don't you?" I say, slamming the tiny locker

183

closed and locking it.

Marcas' smile widens.

Traveling around Marcas' leg, Tax sniffs and scratches at his shoe, as if something is hiding underneath. "Tax,no!" I pull him away by the leash, but he won't budge.

"Is this your dog?" Marcas asks, surprised. Crouching down, he pets Tax's head and lets him lick his fingers and sniff his face. Tax then tries to jump on him. "Whoa, boy. He's so friendly!"

"Today he is," I say, pulling on the leash again, but the dog refuses to obey. "He doesn't usually like strangers. Tax, down!"

"He's all right." Marcas smiles. "Hey there, Tax," he coos, stroking Tax's back as the dog sits.

Marcas is being so gentle with Tax that I wonder if I could be wrong about him after all. Had I misjudged him?

"Tax—that's an interesting name. How'd you come up with it?" he asks as he holds the front door open for me to walk through.

As we step into the afternoon sun, I chuckle. "He was a birthday present from my taxidermy-loving grandpa when I was about ten."

Marcas' face lights up in surprise. "Oh really?"

I shrug in affirmation. "Yeah, he collected all

sorts of animals and kept them in his den. You know, the typical Montana mountain man type. He'd spend hours telling me made-up stories about each one."

"That sounds nice."

My grin widens, having suddenly missed my grandfather even more. "It was. One afternoon I walked through the door and saw a puppy on his lap. I thought it was stuffed. Who wouldn't, right?"

"Of course!" Marcas agrees happily.

"Obviously, he wasn't, but the name sort of stuck after that." I smile, trying to hide the embarrassment of my childhood antics.

As Marcas laughs, his eyes dance. "I like it! Somehow fits."

"Why, because I'm odd?" I tease.

He gives a sort of playful smirk. "You said it."

And we laugh again. It helps to relieve my nerves.

"So, what are you two up to today?" Marcas asks as he dusts the paw prints off his pants he now sees in the light of day.

"Getting this," I say, holding up my mail.

Eyeing my magazine, he grins. "Interesting. Didn't pin you as the celebrity gossip type."

"Jamie thinks I need to be 'enlightened,'" I say,

using air quotes. "She got me a subscription for my birthday last year."

"Ah, right. Makes sense," Marcas agrees as he grabs the door for someone wanting through to their post office box.

"What about you? You out with your brothers?"

"Nah, they're around somewhere. Had to ditch them for a while. Their bickering was getting on my nerves."

I laugh. "I can see that happening."

"Hey, are you busy right now? Want to get some food or something?"

"Uh, yeah, sure. Actually, I was headed to get a smoothie," I say, turning to walk in that direction. "You're welcome to come."

He falls in stride with me down a block to the Bev Café on the main street. We go inside while Tax sits out under the shade of the awning.

Marcas orders first, then motions for me to do the same.

"Oh, no, you go ahead," I say, putting my hair behind my ear.

"Really, it's the least I can do after crashing your plans last night."

Giving a shrug and a hesitant smile, I order then we sit across from each other at a round table by the window to wait.

"You know, you didn't have to do that," I say with a smile. "But thank you."

He grins. "I wanted to."

His smile makes me nervous and excited. And I can't stop the heat from rising to my cheeks.

"Well, anyway, I'm glad you decided to come with us last night. It was fun."

"It was, wasn't it?" This time, when he smiles, two tiny dimples sink into his cheeks that I hadn't noticed before. They are like little, priceless hidden treasures, and the thrill of uncovering more takes me over.

When they call our number from the counter, Marcas gets our drinks and hands mine over with a frown of disgust.

"What?"

"Is that even any good? It looks like blended grass."

I laugh out loud. "Looks can be deceiving. Want a taste?" I say, holding it up.

Backing away like I'm holding something decaying, he chuckles. "I think I'm good."

I take a long sip. The bitter yet sweet taste of chocolate and strawberries melts in my mouth and travels to the pit of my empty stomach, soothing the hungry beast who lives there.

"So, how's your arm?" he asks.

Sucking smoothie down the wrong tube, I start coughing profusely. Not getting air between coughs, I hold up a finger for him to wait a sec.

"You all right?" He pats my back gently, which makes me laugh and cough at the same time.

I nod and try to choke out the word "sorry" as I cough into my napkin. My throat burns. "It hurt yesterday," I finally croak out, "but not so much today." Heaving a heavy breath, I finally breathe without a cough to stifle it away. "Now that I think of it—" I stop to clear my throat. "I forgot to take something for it today," I add with a quick cough.

He can't help but laugh at how I can't stop coughing.

"That's good. Means you're a fast healer. I was sorry to hear what happened."

"Really?" I finally say without a cough to interrupt me. "What exactly did you hear?"

"Niall said you encountered—" he pauses to scan the café for anyone close enough to overhear. Then, leaning close, he whispers, "wolves," before sitting back, an alluring smile on his lips. "I can't say I've ever heard of them being in the area."

"Not as long as I've lived here."

Marcas blows on his hot drink and takes a cautious sip before saying, "Niall said some of them protected you. Why do you think that is?"

"I can't say," I say blankly. The memory plays through my mind again, and even now, I can't find an answer. "All I know is they could have killed me if they had wanted to. I owe them my life." And then I pause, also remembering who else has saved me recently from imminent danger. "Hey, listen, Marcas, about the thing with Brad."

"Shae, there's no need."

"I know, but I just—"

"Shae," he says firmly, reaching over to take my hand and hold it on the table.

His eyes look into mine. Looking past their spectacular sea of green beauty, I can also see a deep concern for me, and it catches me off guard.

"Guys like that, they bully, manipulate, and ultimately force women, and it's wrong!" His tone is calm, yet his hand trembles with anger in mine. "If he ever comes near you again, I swear, I'll—"

"He won't," I reassure him, knowing it holds about as much guarantee as a popsicle not melting in hundred-degree heat. But I don't know how else to handle the worry I see in his eyes.

His thumb caresses my hand, while a troubled

smile rests on his perfect lips, as if it holds the weight of the world.

His words and actions make me feel strange, almost eager to believe this show of concern is real. And his touch, soft and gentle, sends electric pulses streaming through my fingers. Part of me wishes he would never let go.

As if reading my thoughts, he slowly releases my hand and takes a drink.

I nervously tap my straw on the bottom of my cup and watch him, his eyes flashing with the occasional bouts of sadness.

"How come I haven't seen you around?" Marcas finally asks.

"Probably because I haven't been around to be seen," I say, smiling. "I just moved back from Seattle."

"Oh, that's right; I remember Finn saying something about that. Seattle's pretty great! Why'd you end up leaving?"

"Oh, you've been?"

He nods.

"I liked it, too, but something sort of came up, and I decided it was time to come home."

"Work-related?" he asks, curiosity flashing in his eyes. "Relationship troubles?"

"Something like that," I say as my cheeks flush pink. "Something tells me you might know a little about that."

He frowns. "That was pretty awkward last night, wasn't it? Sorry about that."

"Don't be. I get it," I add, watching him fidget with his cup on the table.

We fall silent again.

"So, why'd you guys move to P-burg?" I ask eagerly. "It's not like there's a lot of jobs around here."

He shifts in his seat and stares out the window.

"Sorry, I didn't mean to pry."

"Oh, no, it's not that." He looks at me and smiles. "It's just family stuff and not very interesting. You'll come to find nothing about me really is." Then he gulps down the last of his drink, tipping the cup high to empty it before setting it on the table. "What about you? You find a job yet?"

With narrowed eyes, I smirk at him. Was Marcas checking up on me?

"Jamie told Finn you were looking."

"Ah, yeah, well, the search ended before it began."

"I tried to help Niall find one but came up empty too."

"The high school kids usually get the good ones pretty quick; unless you're up for hard labor or traveling to another town."

"Niall? Hard work? I think he's allergic," Marcas says seriously, yet he smiles.

Then we both laugh.

"What about family? You have any siblings?" he asks more intently as he leans closer to me, putting his arms on the table.

"Nope, it's just my parents and me. I'm fine with it, though; I have Jamie. She's as close as any sister would be."

"How long have you two been friends?"

"Since kindergarten." I smile. "Actually, that's also a pretty funny story."

"I'm intrigued." He grins and moves even closer, our hands practically touching again in the center of the table.

"This one kid, obnoxious as hell, decided it would be funny to squirt glue in my hair. You should have seen Jamie. She grabbed him by the hair so tight that he started kicking and screaming; he made so much noise the teacher came running. But Jamie held tight, insisting he apologized and meant it, or she wouldn't budge. And we've been best buds ever since."

Marcas lets out a boisterous laugh. "Damn, that girl is a firecracker. Remind me never to get on her bad side."

I laugh, too, knowing how true it is.

"It must be nice having such a friend," he says, with a hint of sadness.

"Definitely never dull. But you have friends like that, too, right?"

He scrunches his face as if unsure of it. "Yeah, but it's been years since we've seen each other. I guess it's more about finding the time. We're both kept busy, and it doesn't help that he lives so far away."

"I know what you mean. Living in Seattle, I hardly ever saw Jamie. Between work and school, trips back were so hard when I couldn't stay long," I say sadly, remembering how awful it made me feel not visiting much. "You know, I bet you could always plan to see him when you're done here, right?"

"Maybe, but I'm not sure how long we'll stay. The job we're doing now is tougher than expected; it could take a few more months."

"Months? What are you doing, building a house?" I joke, not expecting an answer.

His lips curl up at the edges, but he tries to

force them back as if he could hide such a gorgeous smile from me.

"Anyway, I guess you guys sticking around wouldn't be the worst thing to happen." I shoot him a shy smile, my cheeks turning rosy and hot.

"Yeah, I guess not." He smiles, too, the tiny dimples appearing again. But then his phone buzzes on the table, and they disappear. "Sorry, I need to get this." He quickly exits through the front door and stands with his back to the window. His muffled voice bounces off the window, but I can't make any words out.

Tax gets up and nudges his head against Marcas' leg. Then, while holding his phone to his ear, Marcas reaches down and casually scratches Tax's ears with his other hand like it's the most natural thing in the world.

So full of girlish giddiness, I cannot pry my eyes away as I ogle Marcas through the window.

The smile on my face expands as I recall how the afternoon has played out. Who knew I would be hanging out with Marcas, the same guy who ripped my head off for meddling in his family business less than twenty-four hours ago? Yet something has changed in him; I almost can't believe he is the same guy.

Marcas hangs up the phone, puts it in his back pocket, then turns and smiles at me through the window.

Embarrassed for being caught red-handed watching him, I wave and hide my reddening cheeks before he comes back into the café and over to the table.

"Everything okay?"

"Actually, something's come up, and I need to get going."

"Shoot. Well, thanks for talking with me." I hold up my cup and smile. "And for the cow feed."

He laughs, his eyes sparkling. "Anytime." Then he walks to the door. After he opens it, he looks over his shoulder at me.

"Shae," he says quietly.

I look at him eagerly.

"It was nice seeing you today."

The alluring smile on his lips sends a thrill of excitement through my body.

"See you around, Marcas."

His smile widens. "Definitely!"

*   *   *

Three of the four walls in the gigantic candy store have every sugary treat imaginable, enough to

195

satisfy anyone's hankering. Glass jars line every shelf. And no matter how many times I move through the store, I can always find something I've never had before.

While perusing, I remove the shiny, metal lid off a jar, grab several sugar-covered gummy O's with metal pincher prongs, and add them to my bag. As I move to the next section, a noisy group of tourists enters the store, heading straight to the free salt water taffy samples at the counter's end. Among them are a few familiar faces.

"Hey, what are you guys doing here?" I say as Niall, Sam, Finn, and Marcas walk over.

"Candy," Sam says with a wink and then makes a beeline for the wall of chocolate.

"Picking a little something up for Jamie," Finn says in passing as he walks to the barrels of candy in the center of the room.

"Had a sudden desire for free taffy, did ya?" I say as Niall stuffs a second piece in his mouth before finishing the first. With puffed cheeks, he puts his arms around me, smelling of fruit and spice.

"Hey," Marcas says to me, smiling.

Letting me go, Niall winks, then picks up a small metal shovel and multiple bags to fill before joining his brothers on their goodies quest.

I look at Marcas skeptically, "You agreed to an outing—for candy?" I snicker. "What, are you, like, five or something?"

He eyes my hand. "It seems we're not the only ones."

"I have no idea what you are referring to." I laugh and hide my bag behind my back.

"Oh, so you came in here to not buy candy?" He chuckles. "I see; makes perfect sense."

Suppressing a laugh, I smile. "Possibly."

He moves to the closest barrel full of miniature caramelized peanut butter hard candies, pressed candy necklaces, taffies, and an array of sparkly, wrapped soft-centered candies and grabs a handful.

"This makes my teeth hurt just looking at it."

"What, you don't eat sugar?"

"I didn't say that." He grins. "I just dislike visiting the dentist more."

"That's fair," I respond, chuckling. "So, then, what's your favorite?"

The corners of his lips curl up like he's keeping a secret.

"What, you think I'll copy you or something?" I say, playfully narrowing my eyes at him. "Sorry, but nothing beats popcorn-flavored jelly beans."

"Is that what you're hiding back there?" he guesses, trying to peek behind me.

"Actually, it's for my mom," I say, bringing the bag around. "Every once in a while, I stop by with something she likes."

"Mo Chroi." He pouts. "That's so thoughtful. Now I almost feel bad for teasing you." Then he exposes a playful yet sweet smile. "Almost."

"You better feel bad!" I counter with a laugh, noticing the particular phrase he used, making me wonder what it could mean.

Marcas casually moves to the wall. "It appears I keep running into you," he says while eyeballing the rows of colored gumballs in jars on the shelf.

"I know; are you following me or something?" I josh doing my own search for candy.

His body stiffens then relaxes back into a casual stance. "What if it's you following me?" He grins while taking the lid off a container, then scoops some candy and puts it in his bag.

"I was in here first, remember?" I grin.

A soft, sprightly smirk appears on his face. "Right."

"Seriously, though, it can't be a coincidence we keep meeting up like this, can it?" I say as I think it.

With the lift of an eyebrow, his grin grows more

prominent. "You know what they say; there's no such thing as a coincidence."

I can't tell if he is serious, but my heart stutters at the thought of him wanting to bump into me again today.

"Well, whatever you want to call it, the other day was nice," I say, and try to hide the smile that wants to shine on my face for the whole world to see.

When he looks at me, his green eyes shimmer with the same genuine happiness that mine do. "Agreed. Not a bad way to spend an afternoon at all."

"Are you fr—"

"Oops, sorry," Niall says, reaching for some sour-flavored bears in front of us. "Just gonna grab this here," he grunts, ". . .and then get out of your way."

"Nice, Niall," Marcas says, a little annoyed as he watches him walk away. "Sorry, you were saying?"

Chickening out, I just smile. "It was nothing."

"Marcas, you done yet? We got to go," Sam calls from the register.

"One sec," he yells back. Again, his dimples appear, and my heart melts. "As always, a pleasure seeing you, Shae!"

"You, too, Marcas," I say, unable to hold back the smile on my lips.

Marcas then goes to the register, pays for their things, and walks out the doors. Before following, Niall waves goodbye to me.

As I finish choosing more gummies to put in my bag, butterflies swarm excitedly in my stomach as I think of Marcas and our little chat. However juvenile the conversation seemed, it felt so natural, so effortless to interact with him now. I blame the talk we had the other day at the smoothie shop, and I have never felt so thankful for such a fortuitous opportunity. And yet, something I saw in his eyes when I mentioned our spontaneous meetings makes me think they are not as accidental as they appear. Believing it could be true sends my heart into a sputtering frenzy in my chest.

Having paid for my stuff, I step up to my car parked out in front of the shop and notice a small bag tied with a yellow ribbon resting on the windshield. In it are red circle candies and yellow and white spotted jelly beans.

I quickly look for who could have left it but find no one around.

CHAPTER 10

MORE QUESTIONS THAN ANSWERS

The words on the page blur and are as fuzzy as the thoughts in my head. Twenty minutes have passed, and I have nothing but a kinked back to show for it. Not a page of progress has been made.

As I stretch my arms up, my back pops in three places, then in my neck as I move it from side to side. Adjusting my position on the carpet, I try to focus on the page again as I absentmindedly pop another candy in my mouth. The red ones aren't half bad.

Tax breathes deeply at my feet. Soon I am

watching him rather than reading.

With a huff, I close the book, its pages snapping together, and smoothly stroke the top of Tax's head. He lifts it, smacks his lips, and yawns as I play with his soft ears.

A dark shadow passes over the window. Traveling across the living room floor, its darkness brings a wave of coolness. Bleak, sinister clouds have gathered in the sky, leaving the day dreary. It has been threatening to rain for days, and now, giant, marble-sized raindrops bong and plink on the metal roof, the earthy smell of rain in the air.

The rain never bothered me much, which was why I had adapted so well to Seattle and its perpetual wet season. Days like this make me feel like I am there again, enjoying the coolness of the summer rain. I refuse to regret that part of my past.

Not caring if I get wet, I put my hair in a messy bun, then grab my waterproof jacket and umbrella from the closet and my wallet from the chair in the living room.

Rain drizzles down in thick, heavy droplets as I move outside. The streets are barren except for the occasional car passing by. For the fun of it, drivers purposefully drive their vehicles through the large puddles, splashing water high into the air.

On Baker Street, I enter the front doors of the library. The large, open room is dark and gloomy from the clouds overhead, obstructing the sun from shining through the window storefront. It is also empty inside and quiet like I hoped it would be.

In the fiction section, on the other side of the new release display, I pick a random book off the shelf and leaf through the pages, skimming the dialog and reading the vague synopsis on the sleeve.

After spending two blissful hours engrossed in fiction, I make my selection and move to the self-checkout computers.

Double-wrapped in plastic, the books rest under my arm as I juggle opening the umbrella and the door before going back out into the rain. Down the street and around the corner, I stop outside Celie's. Shaking the water from the umbrella, I peer through the foggy window. Not a person to be seen.

Inside, the warmth wraps around me like a comfy blanket, heating my body from the wetness outside. My cheeks, cool to the touch, burn as the warm air caresses them. I take off my jacket and sit at my usual table by the window. Water droplets land on the table. I wipe them away with my shirt sleeve as I settle into my seat.

"Hey, I just saw your mom," Judy says as she places the silverware bundle next to my books.

I smile. "Oh yeah? Probably picking up lunch for my dad."

She glances out the window. "Nasty weather out there, isn't it? Cold like winter."

I nod. "Glad it's after the fourth and not before."

"Very true." She glances at the door. "Take a seat anywhere, and I'll be with you in a minute," she calls to someone coming inside, then she looks back at me. "So, what'll it be then, sweetie?"

"Some hot chocolate, please."

Smiling, she writes it down on her pad and then walks away, while I grab my book and turn to the first page.

Wintery-type weather always makes me crave a good book and a tasty, hot beverage; Celie's cocoa is the best. And having never read my recently acquired book, hopefully, this time, I can concentrate enough to enjoy both.

Judy returns shortly with a large, steaming mug of cocoa full to the brim, with whipped cream piled high and chocolate shaving on top. I can feel the hot liquid travel down my throat and into my empty stomach, warming me from the inside out as I sip it down.

Judy sets a menu and a slender glass of ice water on the table. "Got a new book there, I see." She winks. "I'll leave you to it, then, and be back in a bit for your order."

Relaxing in, I begin to read.

I am one chapter down and about to start the second when I hear a familiar voice ask, "Reading anything interesting?"

Over the top of the page, I see a wet-haired Marcas standing with his hands in his jeans pockets.

"Hey!" I smile as my stomach whirls with excitement.

He responds with a warm smile as he shakes his hair free of rain. "Mind if I join you?" He gestures to the empty seat across from me.

While I motion for him to sit, I notice his drenched light-blue shirt clinging to his muscular chest, and my temperature rises.

"So, you're just out for some fun in the rain?" I ask casually as he pulls his chair closer to the table.

He smiles wide. "What? You don't like to bathe in the rain like the rest of us?"

I laugh harder than I should, but I can't help my heart pounding away in my chest like it is. Seeing Marcas so many times, so close together? No way it's a coincidence.

"I was doing some stuff around town with my brothers, and we got stuck in the downpour a few minutes ago."

"Oh, are they coming, too?" I say, my eyes shifting from him to the door and back to his soaked shirt or his muscles—take your pick.

"Finn went to see Jamie, and Sam and Niall had something else to do. So, it's just me. I hope that's all right." He grabs a menu from Judy, who appears out of nowhere. She gives him a flirty smile, exposing yellow teeth, as she bats her fake eyelashes. One half detaches mid-bat, flapping wildly with every blink.

"Fine by me," I say, hiding my face with the menu and trying not to laugh. I didn't want to believe Jamie when she said no matter the age, practically every female has been throwing themselves at Marcas and his brothers. But it can hardly be denied when it's happening right in front of me.

As I pretend to be interested in the menu, I try to tame the surge of excitement that swarms within me at the thought of him being here with me out of all the girls.

After Marcas and I order and Judy leaves,

Marcas leans back in his chair and sighs. A gentle smile is on his lips.

"So, Finn went to see Jamie, huh?" I say coolly. "Took those two long enough to figure things out, didn't it?" I cringe. "Probably shouldn't have said that to you."

"Those two." He shakes his head. "Finn must have started to call her a thousand times but never had the guts to hit the button. I almost did it for him just to make it stop!"

I laugh hard. "Jamie would kill for that kind of intel!"

Pressing his soft, kissable lips together, he smirks, making their edges turn slightly at the corners.

I get lost, staring at his green eyes as he folds his napkin at the corners like a tiny accordion.

"So, why didn't he? Call her, I mean," I inquire, determined to stay focused on the conversation and not get lost in Marcas' good looks.

Marcas shrugs. "He's a tough kid but lousy with rejection."

"Jamie is intimidating, but no one ever said she was any kind of subtle. She wanted him to call. He must have known that."

"I shouldn't speak for him." Marcas then

snickers at the irony of the statement. "But I believe he prefers to show how he cares in person rather than talking about it on the phone."

Judy sets our plates in front of us, and I am left to wonder if what Marcas said about Finn is another common Brannon family trait.

I bite into a fry, and the hot potato explodes in my mouth, burning my tongue and throat as I swallow it. Gulping water doesn't seem to ease the pain. The damage is done, so I take a bite of my cheesey tuna melt instead and savor the taste.

"Marcas, tell me something about yourself," I ask, wiping my lips on a napkin.

As he cuts a piece of his medium rare steak off and dips it in the mashed potatoes, he says, "There's not much to tell," and then eats it. "I'm dull, remember?"

I laugh at his proclamation, finding him about as dull as a priceless piece of art.

"Come on, there has to be something. What about family? You have any around here besides your brothers?"

He smiles as if I've thwarted his obvious answer. "They're pretty much scattered all over the place."

"And..."

"What's to tell? I guess we kind of keep to ourselves most of the time. Besides, as I said before, my life's boring. I'd much rather talk about you."

I blush and use the restaurant's door opening as an excuse to look away. He is still watching me when I look back at him.

"That subject's been talked to death now, hasn't it?" I say before popping another fry in my mouth, much cooler this time.

"On the contrary, Mo Chroi."

There it is again! "What is that—that phrase you just said?"

"Mo Chroi?" He grins sheepishly, as if I have caught him doing something he tried to slip by me. "It's something my father used to say to my mother. In turn, she'd say it to us boys. I guess you could call it a term of endearment. Sorry, I must have said it out of habit."

I get the feeling it wasn't a simple slip of the tongue. "It sounds beautiful. What's it mean?"

He looks into my eyes. "My heart." His velvet-sounding voice sends the meaning of it straight to mine, which is palpitating like mad.

"Oh," I say, and drink some water to calm myself. "Well, if you won't talk about family, tell me your interests. What do you like to do?"

"Travel, I guess."

"You mentioned New York before and Seattle; been anywhere else?"

"So many places—too many to name."

I give him a playful glare. He beams back, knowing he is being aloof, and seems to enjoy his ability to keep from telling me anything of real merit.

"All right." He titters. "Let me think. Okay, well, I've been all over Europe; Ireland mostly, but also a lot of Asia, Africa, and Indonesia."

"Wow! You've been to all those places? I've only been to Mexico, and it wasn't even all that exciting. Why'd you go?"

"Work."

"What kind of job takes you to exotic places like Ireland and Asia and then boring old Philipsburg, Montana?"

Marcas' green eyes dance as he laughs boisterously. It is a robust and bold sound that makes me giggle too.

"What? It's a legitimate question!" I chuckle.

He takes a deep breath when he stops laughing and then smiles widely. "You don't give up, do you?"

My cheeks burn, but it doesn't stop me from

grinning smugly.

"I guess it's like any business, really; sometimes the boss has to travel to job sites," he says with a sigh, "to make sure things are running smoothly, of course."

"I see." My eyes narrow; his answer is as vague as they come.

"Wasn't the answer you were looking for, was it?" The corners of his mouth turn upward, scrunching his cheeks as he reaches across the table and places his hand on my arm.

My heart jumps around in my chest. I can hardly breathe.

"But it seems to be the only one I'll get."

He laughs again, his dimples making another pleasant appearance.

Suddenly, his eyes shift to the window directly behind me. His body tenses; the dreamy smile disappears as he removes his hand from my arm. The door to the restaurant opens as if forced by a gust of violent wind.

"Let me tell him," Sam growls, shoving elbows with his brothers on the way to our table.

Niall shoves him just as aggressively back. "Stop it; I need to explain what happened."

"Guys, knock it off," Finn whispers harshly,

looking at me, a *sorry for the interruption* type of look on his face as they walk up to us. Every inch of their clothes is drenched.

"Look, man, it's not my fault," Sam says to Finn and Marcas. "Doofus over there." —he motions to Niall with his head—"wasn't paying attention, and we lost—" He stops mid-sentence and glances at me. ". . .it."

Wide-eyed and on the brink of tears, Niall clears his throat, his chin trembling.

"I'm sorry, Marcas; I didn't mean to. I-I looked away for a second."

Marcas slams his tightly-fisted hand onto the tabletop, making their bickering abruptly stop. The boom startles me too.

"I don't care what happened. I gave you one job to do—one! And you—"

Niall gulps down a sob. "I'm sorry, Marcas, please don't—"

Marcas glares at him, anger rippling in his eyes.

"We don't have time for this. We need to fix it now before it gets any worse," Marcas says harshly. Then he looks at me. His eyes do not quite reach mine. "I'm sorry, but I have to go. Apparently, my brothers can't handle things on their own."

"No, go; it's fine, really," I say hurriedly, the

eerie calmness to his voice unnerving me.

Giving a forceful, disingenuous smile, he scoots the chair back and stands as he throws his napkin on the table. Then, hurrying to the counter, he pays for his lunch and leaves, never looking back.

Dumfounded, I watch as they walk across the street and then stop. With rain showering down on them, they start arguing again. This time, it appears Marcas is doing most of the talking. Suddenly, Sam pushes Niall, and they start yelling at each other. Marcas grips a piece of each of their shirts and says what I can only assume is 'Enough!' Sam folds his arms forcefully while Niall hangs his head down. They both follow Marcas and Finn as they continue down the street. At the alley, past the giant candy shore, they turn and are gone from sight.

Slouched in the chair, I play with a crusty piece of bread on my plate. Marcas' uneaten food across from me is the only proof that the afternoon lunch with him had even happened.

His sudden mood change had been alarming to witness. And I'm not quite sure if I'm all right with it. What could have possibly happened to make him so angry? What did they lose track of? Were they hunting something—the wolves, maybe? Were they poachers? Was this lunch only a ploy to get their whereabouts out of me? The idea that all this could be a secret attempt at extracting information makes me suddenly feel ill.

Determined to find answers, I grab my phone.

Duke's tonight? I type, then hit send.

Definitely! See you at 9. Jamie texts back.

"Excuse me, Judy," I say as she passes by the table, "could I get the check, please?"

She smiles. "Sweetie, your boyfriend already paid for it."

"My who?" I blink.

She scrunches her forehead. "The guy you were having lunch with. Marcas, right? He paid. Just now."

"Oh, he's not my—we're just friends," I say as the thrill of her assumption comes to life inside me.

Her smile of skepticism widens. "Mm-hm."

CHAPTER 11

WITHOUT REASON

The rain continued to fall for the rest of the afternoon and into the evening; one moment, a mist swirled in the air, and the next, it would seep down, drenching everything in sight.

Duke's parking lot is packed. The only spot remaining is behind the building in the far back corner under a dimly lit street lamp. Not ideal, but better than down the road.

Using my clutch purse as an umbrella, I slam the car door shut and dash for the overhang protecting the gravel walkway to the back door.

When the door to Duke's opens, a wave of hot air rushes at my face, smelling of musty alcohol, stale air, and cheap perfume.

Having been driven in like cattle to escape the rain, people scatter the room. Standing in the doorway and blocking walkways, they force me to squeeze past. When I finally reach the bar, a bottle-red-haired girl is behind the counter with a pierced septum and tattoos running the length of both arms. I ask where Trent is, and she barks back loudly, "Off fer the night," and then asks what I want to drink. Wanting a clear mind, I smile and call for a glass of tonic and bitters. She snubs her petite-ringed nose at me then turns to make it.

While taking sips of the cold drink, I scan the bar and dance floor. Jamie soon comes in the front doors, waving her arms high into the air over the crowd. As she forces her way toward me, a short, stout guy and the gorgeous brunette he starts talking to block Jamie's path. With a quick sidestep, Jamie diverts around the pool tables instead.

"Man, this place is crazy," she yells as she rearranges her chest in her turquoise halter top.

"That another new outfit?" I ask, not surprised in the least if it is but worried she doesn't quite grasp the concept of saving up for college.

Jamie nods enthusiastically, a smile forming on her glossy red lips. She twirls around in a circle, showing off the short black mini skirt and matching knee-high black leather boots. Wobbling off balance, she knocks into a guy standing directly behind us. He smiles widely and motions to the dance floor with his head.

She shakes her head and yells over the music, "Waiting for someone!"

Giving a look of chagrin, he walks away.

"Well, look at you!" She grins as she inspects me closer. "All snazzy in that sexy, spaghetti-strap dress I gave you. It's about time you wore it. So, what's the occasion?"

"Weren't you nagging at me just the other day to make an effort?" I say pointedly.

"That is true." She laughs as she raises her eyebrows while stepping on her tiptoes to see over the hordes of people. "If only that were the real reason. You're wanting to run into someone tonight, aren't you?" she adds over her shoulder.

"Hardly," I say, looking away to hide the pink on my cheeks.

Jamie abruptly grabs my arm and pulls me through the crowd.

"Is Finn coming?" I ask as we stop in the back

corner and sit at the recently emptied table Jamie spotted from across the room. Eyes like a hawk, this one has.

"I'm not sure. He's doing something with the boys but will try to make it if he can."

I swallow the sudden lump in my throat. "Hey, so you've spent a lot of time with those guys, right?"

She nods.

"Have you noticed anything odd about them?"

She scrunches her brow for a moment. "Sam wears the same socks two days in a row. Is that what you mean? Because that's just gross." She adds a stink face to reiterate how disgusting it is.

"Ew, really?"

She affirms it with a laugh.

Shaking the disturbing thought from my mind, I try again. "No, I mean, more like secretive kind of stuff?"

"Secrets? Shae, what's this about?"

"I've just noticed things—as I'm sure you have too. I mean, what do they do all day, and why won't they talk about it?"

"Oh, that? I figured it was just the family business," she says as her eyes revert toward the front doors when she sees someone resembling

Finn walk in. When it isn't, she frowns and keeps looking.

"And you never wondered what that is exactly? Why they won't even talk about it? Or where they disappear to all the time?"

"You've thought a lot about this, haven't you?" she says, turning to me.

"Not that much," I lie.

"Why do you care so much about it anyway?" she asks, a look of concern in her eyes.

"I don't *care,* care; I'm just a little concerned. You don't think they are doing anything illegal, do you?"

Jamie laughs robustly and then wipes the pooling tears from under her eyes.

"You kill me, Shae. Have you seen my boyfriend, Mr. Boy Scout?" She laughs again because I guess my humiliation for assuming such a thing wasn't driven home enough with the first stint of laughter.

"Fine, maybe not illegal, but something they shouldn't be doing."

Jamie stops laughing and looks at me. "No. No way they are mixed up with anything remotely controversial. Why would you even suggest such a thing?"

"It's just that when I was having lunch with

Marcas, his brothers—"

"Wait!" She clutches my arm tightly. "You had lunch with Marcas and didn't call me?"

"Calm down. It wasn't a big deal. It just sort of happened," I say dismissively, but my cheeks still burn warm.

"Uh, yeah, it is! You, out with someone, this is huge!"

"Not as much as you're making it," I say, giving a stern stare.

"So, what was he wearing? How did he act—did he kiss you?"

"Hah, like he'd walk up and go, *'Oh hey, Shae, how's it going? And by the way, kissy-kissy!'*" I mock, using a man's voice then roll my eyes.

"Please, guys do that to me all the time—did, I mean did."

"Says the girl who could bat her luscious lashes and make all the men bow at her feet."

"Whatever!" she says, scrunching her nose. "But admit it. Deep down, you wanted him to kiss you. And don't you dare tell me that Marcas hanging out with you is no big deal because I saw you two the other day at the carnival." She eyes me cynically. "And on the blanket. I see the way he looks at you!"

I swallow hard, unsure if I should hold on to

such hope and believe what she says is true.

"Yeah, but we were all there. And lunch was just—" I sigh because what was lunch? Unexpected, fun, exhilarating, and one of the best afternoons I've had in a long time. Marcas' dimples and smiling, green eyes make my heart pound just thinking about them. But it's all too new—too unpredictable, and could easily be jinxed before it has a chance to evolve.

"Lunch was two people eating and talking. That's it. Besides, like I was trying to explain, the boys came and dragged him away. Something about losing track of something, or whatever."

"Strange," Jamie says contemplatively.

"Right? Thank you." Finally, confirmation that I am not losing my mind.

"Finn did say Marcas swore off dating anyone else from around here," she says, watching the dance floor.

"That's not what I—" then I realized what she said. "Finn said that?" Anxious, I play with my glass, suddenly finding the condensation on the side fascinating.

Jamie nods slowly. "But still, guys like him don't just go around having lunch all willy-nilly with any girl. It has to mean something."

221

"Yeah, that he's hungry and prefers company to eating alone."

"Stop that! Maybe he changed his mind!"

I take a moment to ponder it, but the more I think about it, the more my stomach turns with angst.

Marcas' actions over the past several days have suggested as much. But what if I've misread them, finding feelings where there aren't any? It wouldn't be the first time.

But of all the girls, how could I believe someone like him would choose me? Boring, emotional baggage-wielding me. Could I be wrong about all of it after all?

The corners of my mouth droop. "Anyway, there's no sense swooning over someone who doesn't even want to date me." I can feel a hole in my stomach getting bigger.

"Ah-ha, I knew it; you do like him!" she screeches loudly, pointing her finger at me. "He's who you're waiting for!"

"Shh!" I hiss, feeling my cheeks burning.

"So, what are you going to do? Talk to him?"

"No! I don't know."

"I could ask him—"

"Don't you dare!" I say, grabbing her arm and

squeezing it tight. "Promise you won't!"

"Fine," she cringes, removing my grip. "I won't, but I swear he likes you back." Then she flinches, her phone vibrating in her hand. "It's Finn. They're on their way in." She beams excitedly, then falters. "Oh, but they might not stay long, though. I guess it was a rough day."

"Bummer. And I was so looking forward to watching you guys play kissy face all night," I say with a snide grin.

"Ha, ha." She rolls her eyes, jumps out of the seat, and swims her way through the crowd. Finn had just walked through the door with Sam.

Finn stays where Jamie had tackled him, blocking everyone coming in, while Sam heads for the pool tables. Half the girls sitting at the bar turn their heads, following his every move.

I smile at their desperation. Then I realize I'm just like them, heart pounding in my chest with anticipation for who's to come through the door next.

It is useless to deny the feelings swarming inside me. I like Marcas—a lot. And I want him to like me, too. And yet the vulnerability I feel scares me more than anything else I have dealt with lately.

In expectation, I watch the door. My breathing

speeds up when it opens. Two girls in shorts and bandanas for shirts walk through. Marcas follows right behind them.

His hair, messy and wet from the rain, still looks fantastic. Even from here, I can see the raindrops scattered on his gray V-neck shirt clinging to his body.

He sits at the counter and starts talking with the red-headed bartender. She leans closer to him and touches his arm. Then, as she flips her hair back, she laughs. Jealousy burns in my chest. And like some love-sick puppy, I can't stop staring at the two of them. At least not until someone steps in front of me, blocking my view.

"Maggie, do you mind?" I say, trying to look around her, but now I can't even see past the people behind her.

"As a matter of fact, I do. We need to talk."

"Uh, no, we don't!"

"Just—will you stop being annoying for half a second and listen to me?"

Folding my arms across my chest, I stare hard at her.

"Look, about the other day . . . I guess I was kind of . . . you know . . . rude or whatever." She rolls her eyes. "So, I figured I'd, you know, say

224

something about it."

"What?" I say, narrowing my eyes.

Her face turns beet red with wrath, but then her eyes soften as she lets out a long breath. "Look, what I'm trying to say is that—I may have acted kind of possessive when I didn't have the right to."

"You mean because you and Marcas aren't dating like you made it seem?" I state bluntly with satisfaction.

"Ugh, yes. And you know, you weren't very nice before, either."

"Seriously? You want me to apologize to you? You're the one who attacked me, remember?"

"Shae—grr, you make me so—" She stops and only regains composure after more deep breaths. "Look, this isn't how I wanted things to go." She lets out a soft chuckle. "Guess I'm no good at these kinds of things."

Holy crap, is this for real? Maggie feels bad for something awful she's done! Maybe she wasn't lying when she told Marcas she wanted to be better.

"Suppose not," I say, smiling at the irony of her statement.

She suddenly glares. "Don't make fun."

"Maggie, I didn't—I just understand how hard it is, that's all." This time, my eyes mirror the sincerity of my meaning.

Her eyes narrow. "Don't patronize me by pretending to be nice. We're not friends. I'm only here because my therapist said to."

"I wasn't pretending, though maybe I should have thought twice about it," I say heatedly. "Why bother to apologize if you don't even mean it?"

She gives a snide huff. "I didn't mean it like that." But then her resentment dissolves slightly. "I do care . . . about being sorry. Look, I was wrong before, and I know that now, so."

With my eyebrows raised, I wait for her to actually say the words *'I'm sorry,'* but then I'm not surprised when she doesn't.

"So, do you?" Her eyes shift between me and the floor. "Accept my apology . . . for everything?"

"I mean, it's great that you're trying, really it is, but do you even feel bad for all the *other* times you were horrible to me?"

She watches two girls walk by before looking at me again. "I'd say yes, but we both know I'd be lying. I can't take back what I can't even remember."

Aggravation pricks at me, but I hold it in.

"No, but you know how you were, Maggie. You may not remember what you did, but you still did it. I don't know if I can forgive that."

For the first time in my life, I am witnessing something I would have sworn could never happen. A single tear slowly trickles down her cheek. She nods and sniffs. "Fair enough." Then she wipes the tear away.

Call it empathy or guilt, but whatever it is, I suddenly feel a whole lot of it. Not a single person on earth would fault me for not wanting to forgive her. But it just isn't like me. No matter how hurtful she can be, she is also trying to change. And I know how hard that can be, especially for someone like her.

"All right, all right, fine. Let's just agree to move on. You stay in your lane and me in mine."

With half a smile, her countenance perks up. "Sounds fair. But this doesn't mean we're friends or anything, right?" she adds hurriedly.

"Hardly!" I smile.

Nodding her head, she gives an honest smile and then turns on her high heels. As she walks away, the crowd parts, exposing a view of Marcas sitting at the bar.

Making my way across the room, I look for Jamie and Finn but find neither, though I do see Niall coming in from outside. He walks down the small stairs to the pool tables and Sam. When he sees me, he waves, though it lacks its usual luster. Nevertheless, I am happy to see he at least came.

When I reach the bar, hordes of girls occupy most of the space around Marcas. Why am I not surprised? I have to squish between them to get close enough to tap his shoulder.

The dorkishly large smile on my face broadens as Marcas swivels around in his chair.

His eyes narrow in on me, and without so much as a word, he turns back around.

A heavy ache forms in my chest. It travels like a bag of rocks into my stomach.

"Marcas?" I say hesitantly and put my hand on his shoulder. I can feel his body tense up with my touch, yet he does not respond.

"Are you all right? Did something happen?" I ask, trying to surpass the worry I feel. Why is he being like this?

He looks at me from the corner of his eye, then forward again.

Slowly, I remove my hand from his shoulder, and my stomach sinks.

It's me? But I-I didn't do anything!

Suddenly, I feel anger erupting inside me like a pipe bursting on an oil rig, and it cannot be contained.

"What the hell, Marcas?" I growl, grabbing his elbow and pulling, using momentum to make him swivel to face me again. This time I anticipate the look of disgust he gives. "Seriously? Wait—let me guess, I don't exist again for my own good, right?"

"Shae, I really don't want to talk right now," he says over his shoulder as he calmly turns to face the bar again and slowly takes a drink.

I hear whispers from behind me and what I assume are gasps of shock from the girls as they eavesdrop, but I am too heated to care.

"Fine, then say that. Don't-don't ignore me like a child," I hiss through my clenched teeth. I want so badly to rip the glass out of his hand and chuck it across the room, so he'll do something; anything but sit there like that—like he doesn't care.

"Figured it was clear enough," he says flatly, taking another drink.

Sadness attempts to take me over, but I press it down deep. I will not let Marcas shake me. Not this time.

"Why are you being like this?" I bark back and stretch around to see his face. But he remains focused on the wall of endless bottles of alcohol. "Damn it, look at me! I don't underst—"

"What's not to get?" Marcas huffs, looking at

229

me, his green eyes staring almost through me. I feel the cold of his glare like ice on my skin. "I don't want you around me!"

"But what about the other day? Or lunch today, I thought—"

He grunts. "What? You thought we were friends or something? Dating?"

"No, I—Marcas, what happened? What did I do?" Reaching for his arm, I gulp down the lump of helplessness I feel. But he yanks his arm free from me, making me flinch.

"Don't you get it? You're just like every other desperate girl in this damn town. None of you can take a hint," he says, glaring at all the girls listening. They scowl at him and look away.

My eyes pool with tears. I blink them back, but they won't go away.

"It was just lunch. It doesn't mean anything. You and me—" He points to himself and to me. "—we're nothing. Never were and never will be, so go find someone else to stalk." His words, full of spiteful loathing, linger heavily in the air. They hit me like a baseball bat to the gut, punching me so severely I cannot breathe.

How stupid am I to be blinded by him again? To fall for his charm, his good looks, to be sucked into his world only to have it collapse on me without warning!

Through his scowl, his beautiful green eyes seem to laugh at me.

Tears overflow from my eyes and run down my cheeks. I open my mouth to speak, but nothing comes out but pathetic-sounding rasps.

"I have plenty of my own problems, you know!" he adds sharply as he aggressively wipes a drop of water from his forehead. "I don't need any of this—you hanging around all clingy and suffocating me with all your crap. It's irritating, and I can't take it anymore. I can see now why your boyfriend ditched you."

His last words break me. Like daggers, every word stabs my vulnerable heart until nothing is left. I watch his icy, uncaring eyes harden, void of anything but hatred, as I stand there in utter agony. Every ounce of affection I have for him seeps from the wounds he is inflicting.

I want to scream, *'What is wrong with you? What have I done?'* at him, but I know it's not me. It can't be me. I have done nothing wrong!

No—yes, I have. I should have listened to the warnings. I should have known better than to trust him! And now look at what I let happen. He sucked me in, convinced me to open my heart to the idea of finding happiness again, and this is my reward. Betrayal, humiliation, and regret—more regret than I ever thought I could feel.

Unable to control it, I let out a pain-filled, pitiful sob. The room begins to shrink around me. My hands clench into tight fists at my sides. The overwhelming desire to hit him repeatedly, to hurt him as he hurt me, burns like an inferno inside me. But I can't seem to move or speak a word.

I turn away, unwilling to look at him any longer. Niall is standing two feet away, horror in his wide eyes. He moves toward me, his hand outstretched, but I flick it aside and rush past him through the crowd to the back exit. The door swings open; the slam of it hitting the wall outside echoes into the hollow night.

Everything outside is drenched, but the rain has stopped. The cool, damp air rushes at my heated skin like snow on hot ash as I run along the side of the building. Strength leaves me, and I fall against the chilly brick wall. Sobs burst from my chest, huge heaving sobs that just keep coming. My arms squeeze around my ribcage to keep my heart from bursting from it, but the agonizing pain of heartbreak perseveres.

Why? Why would he treat me like that?

Happy images of today flash in my mind, making the sting of their hollowness rip deeper into my heart.

"Hey, you good?" a man asks somewhere down the building.

I ignore him.

"You need some help?" he asks again, now only a few steps away.

Raising my head, I see familiar, haunting eyes staring back at me.

"Shae? What are—you all right?" Brad says, his look of concern turning to surprise.

I nod and sniff, wiping my face. "Yeah, I'm fine."

"Clearly, you're not," he says, trying to put his arm around me.

"I said I'm fine!" I say, shrugging it off me as I turn around.

Dark shadows move around the corner of the building.

"Wow, sweetness, why the tears?" someone else says, stepping closer, their face hidden by the shadows.

"Steve, can't you see Shae's upset?" Brad says.

"This is—this is Shae?" the guy says, surprised,

though it's evident by his over-the-top reaction that he's not. "Damn, Brad, you ain't lyin'. She's lookin' super fine tonight."

As the stranger steps into the halo of the streetlight, I see there are actually two of them, seemingly just as tall and menacing as Brad.

"Dude, you're being insensitive," Brad says, trying to stroke my hair.

Body chills cover me as I realize the danger circling around me like vultures.

"No! Stop," I say, flicking Brad's hand away and taking a step back. "Please, just leave me alone!"

I move through their diminishing circle, but they block me, forcing me back toward Brad.

"Brad, listen, I'm sorry about the other night, but you have to let me leave," I say through tears, my nose stuffed, making the words nasally.

Desperate, I look around for anyone who can stop this, but I find no one—not even a passerby in a car, on the street, or at the other end of the parking lot. And the music inside is too loud to scream over.

My stomach sinks.

The light from the streetlamp starts flickering, darkening parts of Brad's ominous face.

"Shh, don't you go worrying your pretty little

head about that," he coos. "I'm here for you, and we've got all the time in the world."

"Yeah, loverboy inside don't want nothin' to do with you now," Steve says with a laugh.

"Hah, lucky us," the other one says while stepping forward. His disgustedly twisted grin makes me cringe.

Without warning, Brad pushes me against the wall, pinning me to it.

Using my clutch purse, I hit him over and over—his head, arms, and chest—anything I make contact with. But he catches hold of my arm mid-swing and squeezes tight. The splint beneath his grip digs deep into my arm, making me cry out in pain as he hammers my arm against the wall until the purse falls to the ground.

Using an extra amount of aggressiveness, he tries to slide his hand up the bottom of my dress. I scream and try to shove his hand away, but he slams his other hand hard over my mouth. My teeth dig into my lips underneath.

"Hey—don't you scream!"

The sharpness of his tone scares me.

"Come on now, you don't want me to lose my temper, do you?" he adds, his soothing voice returning as if we are having a pleasant conversation. "I wouldn't want to be the reason your pretty face gets all messed up."

I shake my head ever so slightly, my eyes wide with fear. Then, with the tip of his nose, he trails the length of my neck. I try to recoil from it, but his hand over my mouth keeps me from moving. Finally, he lets up on my mouth slightly but doesn't pull away entirely as he caresses my cheek with his hand. Then, inhaling deeply near my ear, he exhales the smell of stale cigarettes and beer on me.

"Now, what were you saying the other day—oh, that's right. You were trying to convince me you weren't up for any fun," he says with a hint of mockery. "But I can clearly see you are now, aren't you?"

Squeezing the tears from my eyes, I let out a small, childish whimper as I again shake my head. Unable to look at his hideous face any longer, I turn away. His friends snicker as they step closer to block us from the view of others.

"Look at me!" Brad growls, squashing my cheeks into my teeth as he forces me to look at him. "You think I made that up?" he hisses, pulling my lips toward his mouth. Even though it hurts so bad that tears well in my eyes, I struggle to keep his lips from mine. To my luck, his grip gives way. He chuckles, but he doesn't sound the slightest bit amused.

"Don't be like that, sweetheart. You'll love them, I promise."

When he comes in for another try, I squirm my head around to keep his lips from finding mine. Determined to take what isn't his, he grabs my face again and squeezes hard to stop me from moving.

The kiss, aggressive and slobbery wet, tastes bitter—of tobacco and alcohol.

When he lets go of me, I can still feel the impression of his strong hand on my cheeks and the weight of his hard kiss on my lips.

He moves to my neck, kissing slowly down to my chest. My body shudders, and he chuckles under his breath.

"I think she likes it, Brad," Steve taunts boastfully.

"You know she does; look at her face," the other friend jeers eagerly.

Brad pulls at one of my dress straps. "Is that right, Shae? Are you finally having fun?" It snaps in his hand, and he lets it fall. "Oops," he snickers. "Lucky for us, your boyfriend isn't around to get in the way again." Then he slithers his finger down my skin. "Or should I say, ex-boyfriend?" He grins

237

evilly.

I cry even harder, knowing how right he is. Marcas will not come this time. That I am sure of.

Mascara stings my eyes as I squeeze them shut tight and wiggle in Brad's grip to get free. Black tears stream down my face.

To keep me pinned to the wall and free up his dirty hands to aggressively rub all over me, he presses his lower body harder against me. In his error, I knee him right in the groin and run as Brad roars loudly with rage and balls over in pain.

"Where do ya think you're going, sweetheart?" Steve grunts as he and the other guy shove me back.

Brad gets up and grabs me by the throat. "You'll pay for that!" he roars as he swings the back of his hand, hitting me square in the cheek.

My face burns like fire, so much it feels numb. Brad strikes again, harder this time. The force of the blow flings me against the wall behind us. My head slams against the hard brick surface. A warm, wet liquid drips from my nose and head as I topple to the gravel below.

Traveling in and out of consciousness, I desperately try to focus through the pain. Darkened images flicker around me through a hazy blur. Warped and distant, like echoes in a tunnel, I hear the scuffing of shoes on the wet gravel. Then a monstrous growl from a man as it ricochets off the wall into the night. As if spoken in another language, the low hums of muddled whispers soon follow.

I am unaware of how much time has passed.

My mind craves rest. Even in my desperation to stay lucid, I know I will eventually have no choice but to give in to the sweet stillness of sleep.

I feel a tug on my body. Someone is moving me. As I sink deeper and deeper, drowning in a swirl of fragmented thoughts, I hear a man's voice, razor-sharp like a knife, slice through to the very center of my consciousness.

"Please don't leave me . . . I can't live without you.

To be continued . . .

Thank you

for taking the time to read my book. I appreciate you and hope you enjoyed reading it as much as I did writing it. I would love to hear your comments, critiques, and most importantly, what parts you enjoyed the most. If you would please take a moment to leave a review on Amazon or Goodreads, it would be greatly appreciated. Then stop by my website, sign up for my newsletter, and tell me more about what you loved and why. I just love hearing all about it.

Amazon Review

Goodreads.com

S.L.McMullin.weebly.com

BY FATE OR BY CHOICE.

Here is a sneak peek into

FATE BY SUNRISE

the next installment in the

SECRETS BY MOONLIGHT SAGA

Amazon Link

—Marcas cups my cheek in his hand and wipes a tear away with his thumb. "Please don't do that. I promise it will be ok."

"Tell me." I gulp down the fear lifting from the pit of my stomach. "What's going on?"

"Shae, I need you to know—my promise to you—I meant to keep it," he says as if he had already failed. "But I also gave my word not to speak of what I am about to, no matter the cost." His green eyes shimmer with concern as he searches mine for understanding, but I am so on edge that I can't even blink. "I promise, I'll tell you everything."

My heart suddenly sputters in my chest. Now. Now I get my answers.

"Those men are here because of me, not Brad," Marcas says quietly.

"You brought them here?" Jamie blurts out, spinning to look at Finn. "You knew who that jerk was and didn't say anything?"

"No! I didn't know they were the same guy!" Finn exclaims.

"Conall has come for the same reason we have, but we did not invite him—had no idea what he had planned to do." Then Marcas looks back at me, his eyes full of sorrow. "I didn't know he would try to hurt you."

"Why are you here, Marcas?" I say, looking into his eyes. "That guy, he said—"

Marcas takes a deep breath. "I knew I'd have to answer that someday." He smiles slightly, his eyebrows subtly raised, yet his voice remains semi-serious.

"Not home builders, I take it?" I smile awkwardly through my unease because, for just one meager second, I want to believe what he is about to tell me is as simple and unscary as a pile of bricks.

The pensive look he gives in return confirms I'm about to be disappointed.

My leg bounces wildly, my heel patting rapidly on the floor to the beat of my heart. I am afraid—afraid of everything changing and having no way of stopping it.

Marcas stands. "What I am about to say will sound absurd, made up even, and probably impossible to believe," then he starts pacing again. "But it is all true."

2

I hold my breath, unsure if I am really ready to hear what he's been wanting to tell me all along.

"No joke, you guys can't tell anyone," Niall chimes.

"Niall, seriously?" Jamie glares.

He snarls back at her, but she ignores him.

"Just say it, Marcas," I say.

Marcas comes to my side, and with the back of his fingers, he strokes my cheek lovingly. "It is hard to explain." His hand comes to rest on my shoulder. "But it has to do with your necklace."

As if signaling *I am here*, the pendant warms against my chest like it had done so many times before.

"My necklace?" I say, feeling it through my shirt, hesitant to reveal it. "What does it have to do with any of this?"

Marcas grins knowingly. "Everything, Shae—it's the very reason my brothers and I are here."—

STEPHANIE L. MCMULLIN

Having had an overactive imagination since birth, Stephanie has finally put her creativity to print. *Secrets By Moonlight* is her first solo published work of fiction. Look for the exciting continuation of the saga in *Fate by Sunrise* to be released in 2023. Stephanie resides in Spanish Fork, Utah with her husband and four children.

www.ingramcontent.com/pod-product-compliance
Lightning Source LLC
Chambersburg PA
CBHW020058180626
46812CB00006B/2385